The New Home

Shauna Leone

Also by Shauna Leone

The Resonant

1

Copyright © Shauna Leone 2023

The right of Shauna Leone to be identified as the Author of the Work has been asserted by her in accordance with the Copyright, Designs and Patents Act 1988

All rights reserved. No part of this publication may be reproduced, stored in a retrieval system, or transmitted, in any form or by any means without the prior written permission of the author, nor be otherwise circulated in any form of binding or cover other than that in which it is published and without a similar condition being imposed on the subsequent purchaser.

All Characters in this publication are fictitious and any resemblance to real persons, living or dead is purely coincidental.

*In Memory of Maggie
My friend at the end of the lane*

Chapter 1

I can't remember the last time I was here, not properly anyway. It was something that I had long buried. Most people have early memories and yet I do not. It had never occurred to me that this was strange. I know I lived here once in this small weather beaten cottage in the West Country at the bottom of a lane to nowhere with my mother and my aunt; all girls together for I do not know who my father was and my mother would never speak of him. I am sure he was never here for even the first years of my life as I am uncertain whether he was ever told about me. At least I have always hoped that he wasn't. It made it easier to explain away the lack of birthday and Christmas cards from the years I do remember. I do know I went to school nearby and I must have played in this garden and walked the coastal path to the beach to go searching in rock pools for all kinds of life, collecting the shells I still have locked away in a box somewhere. I must have gone into the woods that surround me now and played amongst the trees, perhaps trying to climb them, perhaps with friends, perhaps on my own and yet I can visualize none of it. Sometimes I think I may have a memory but then I wonder if it is more my imagination filling in the blanks, making images of the things I have been told happened rather than any real recollection. But like I say it had never really troubled me.

I left here when I was seven; twenty odd years ago.

Now it does bother me slightly. I had expected to return to the cottage and be swamped with images. To have memories which would allow me to finally grieve for my recently deceased aunt and yet there is nothing.

Actually that is a lie. There is something but it is something that I am uncomfortable with. It nags at the corners of my mind but never reveals itself and a sinking feeling comes across me growing into nausea so bad I feel the need to put my hand against the cold stone of the cottage to keep myself from falling to the ground. My heart pounds in my ears and it feels as if someone has replaced my brain with syrup and is now swirling it around.

I take deep breaths and wait for the feeling to pass which it does almost as quickly as it came on. I have been through a lot recently and I am getting used to these panic attacks. They are becoming easier to cope with now I know them for what they are, however that does not mean they are getting any less frequent. Hopefully getting away from it all will help with that.

I sniff in the cold air and blow it out between pursed lips a couple more times. I feel my heart slow and the world once again comes into focus. The eddy that my brain had become fades away and all is calm once more but I keep my hand on the wall, the solidity of the stone making me feel more secure somehow, as I walk around the outside of my new home. Or at least what will be my home for the next couple of weeks until I decide what to do with the place.

It is a simple farm-style cottage, reminiscent of the kind of house a child might draw together with a happy family of stick figures standing outside and a big yellow sun against a line of scribbled blue sky. It sits square with a slate roof, a chimney at the corner and four small windows at the front unlikely to let in much light. I certainly have to strain my eyes to see through them to what lies waiting for me inside; grey lumps of furniture crouch in the shadows but I can work out little else. There is a tangle of vines trailing around the dark oak front door and upper windows which I presume will flower in spring or summer and look beautiful but now it all looks twisted and skeletal and dead. The front garden is a small square patch of overgrown grass. Flower beds border it and although there is nothing growing in them at present I can see some tags with the names of what must be buried there and pictures of what will fill the bare earth before long no doubt. I try to picture my aunt tending them, carefully planting the seeds which she would never see grow but even this simple fantasy evades me as I know so little about her. All is framed by a wooden fence which brambles have attempted to claim, winding their way half up the posts, and a path runs from the door down to a rickety gate which leads out to the pothole riddled lane and then to the woods beyond. It does feel as if winter has gripped this place, strangling it and keeping everything but the grass and brambles from growing or as if everything died here along with my aunt. Hopefully I can breathe some life back into it all and it in turn will breathe some life back into me.

    My mother and Aunt Carol must have been close once to have lived together here with me but something happened and my aunt never visited us in London and we never came back here. I wasn't even sure how to contact her when my mother was diagnosed with cancer two years ago and died three months later. I sent a letter to this address hoping that my aunt still lived here but heard nothing. I guess I didn't really expect to and didn't think too much of it at the time. My mother would hardly talk about my aunt and I never gave her much thought. Out of sight out of mind and with no happy memories, no memories at all, I didn't miss her so it was a surprise to get the solicitor's letter a month ago saying that her entire estate had been left to me. I feel bad I never made it to the funeral now but she died about the time of the incident.

I shake my head at the word incident. It was how it was described though. Such an insipid word for what actually happened.

Now it is my turn to push memories away rather than dig for them. It is getting dark now, the sky low and grey and threatening rain and the wind has picked up. A gust slices through me and I huddle into my coat and sweep my hair from my eyes. It is February and the evenings have the promise of lighter days in them but still it seems that night creeps in much earlier than it should here. Back in London I'd noticed the frost from last week had gone and I saw snowdrops in the neighbour's garden before I left. It made me smile, something I don't seem to have done in a long while. If only I could trade the memories of the past year for those of my lost childhood.

I decide it is getting too late to go into the house tonight and I don't like to admit it but I feel spooked by the place. I can smell fire smoke wafting from a nearby chimney, all woody and spicy and inviting and making me want to curl up in the warm somewhere with a home cooked meal and a large glass of wine. Suddenly I feel very tired and realise that is just what I need after the five hour journey so I make the decision to find a bed and breakfast. I had planned to stay here at the cottage tonight but that now seems a very bad idea so I head back to my car, parked just outside the gate which I have to jiggle a little to release the catch and open just as I did when I arrived. I take one last look at the property, looming raven against an ominous sky, challenging me to come and reveal its secrets of a childhood forgotten. I contemplate it for a moment, still not quite believing that I now own it, before getting in my car and driving back up the lane to the small village I just passed through.

    As I come to the main road I see my preoccupation with finding the cottage wasn't the reason I hardly noticed the village on the way here. There is little of note. A few small shops line the high street. I pass a butchers, a post office and a hair salon among other non-descript stores selling all sorts of bric-a-brac and there is a tiny cafe on the corner advertising freshly baked pasties and all day breakfasts. Only a grocery store is open now, where I see a few teenagers sat on a bench outside, huddled in their hoodies and smoking roll-ups. A church dominates the centre of the village. It seems to have been built on a bank so that it looms over the street, its spire like a preacher keeping a careful eye on his flock. It is flanked by crooked tombstones which look like blackened sharks teeth in the failing light. On the other side of the street there is a pub advertising vacancies in its window, "The Lady of the Lake". The sign has seen better days and the 'e' of the word Lake is hardly legible. The picture on it has a medieval aspect and shows a woman coming out of the water, dark hair flowing over her shoulders and down to her waist, sword held aloft and white gown clinging to her; a nod to all the Arthurian legends around the area. I must have already passed at least five signs for King Arthur's Stone, or King Arthur's Castle or King Arthur's Halls since I crossed into the county, all attempting to lure in tourists with the promise of old legends and magic and probably with the hope that, once there, a crystal or dragon ornament might be purchased in the gift shop and perhaps a cream tea may be indulged in. There don't seem to be many other options of bed and breakfasts on the village's short high street and the pub looks to be cosy enough and just what I need for a night so I park the car on the empty road and head inside as the first drops of rain begin to fall.

    Funny how living in London you tend to become independent, going everywhere in your own little bubble, paying little mind to anyone and they in turn paying little mind to you, everyone too busy with their own lives to take the time to look around. Now I dread walking into a pub on my own. I feel eyes upon me as I push open the heavy door which rattles announcing my entrance far more loudly than I would wish. The warmth inside embraces me but the stares chill at the same time. I clumsily shut the door behind me realising the way the warmth has been so inviting to me, so must the cruel icy wind from outside have been equally uninvited. Maybe the stares weren't so much for me as they were for the winter air, and yet the eyes follow me as I walk to the bar.

    There are a handful of patrons. I try to not pay too much attention to any of them hoping they will repay me the courtesy. The pub is small and only has about five tables with mismatched chairs and benches around them. A log fire crackles in the corner and a pool table dominates most of the space. The ceiling is low with dark beams running across it which are cluttered with hanging tea cups and horse brasses. A juke box is secured to one of the walls though no one has bothered to put any credits on it. Perhaps if they had I wouldn't get the feeling each footstep I take to the bar is being judged as it echoes on the stone floor. Opposite the juke box is a fruit machine flashing with red and orange spirals and promises of jackpots. A proper traditional pub, it reminds me of many drunken nights in Shoreditch back when I was at university, back when everything was so much simpler and, to be honest, what I am remembering feels like another life now. I haven't stepped into a place like this for a while. I know there are still plenty to be found in London but everyone I know seems to favour the trendy wine and cocktail bars lately. I even spy a painting of dogs playing poker above the fireplace and smile to myself. You just don't get that kind of décor enough these days.

Two men sit at the bar. They smell of earth and animals and their muddied boots suggest a hard day's work out on some farm or building site somewhere. It is hard to tell how old they are under their unkempt beards but one of them in a tweed cap may be in his sixties. Grey whiskers poke from his ears and his cheeks, going a little way to disguise the fine purplish veins which spider across his face telling of a lifetime of exposure to the elements or perhaps to the beer which he is now clutching in grimy hands, black lines of ingrained dirt in his finger nails and knuckles. The younger, wearing a beanie, I could imagine being his son or apprentice perhaps, his skin not yet ravaged by the elements but swarthy even in winter though I wonder whether soap and a flannel might reveal a much lighter tone.

They have stopped talking, their half empty pints forgotten for a moment as they study me. I smile politely at them but get no reaction so I avoid any further eye contact as I wait to get served. Instead I notice the white bubbles clinging to the sides of their glasses slowly drifting down into the golden liquid still waiting to be consumed. I stare at it intently, aware that they are staring at me in exactly the same way and for a moment I get lost in the darkness of it. I feel as if the liquid I am looking at is far murkier and deeper than that which the glass contains. It is as if I am sinking in it, drowning…

'Hello, what would you like darlin'?' a voice pulls me back to reality.

The bar maid is smiling. The contrast to the serious and distrustful looks I have received so far in here makes me want to thank her. It seems a sincere greeting too, her rosy cheeked face open and honest with dimples which accentuate her happy countenance. She is all curves with short blond hair pulled into a messy ponytail so that it sprouts out of the band this way and that and her eyes twinkle as if she is easily amused by people. She can't be much older than me and I instantly like her and am sure it is not just because she is the first friendly face I have seen here.

'Um, I saw you had vacancies and was wondering if you had a single room for tonight.'

'Yes I do as a matter of fact. Just want it for tonight?'

'Yes please. I'm meant to be staying at a cottage near here but I just didn't feel like cooking for myself and making a bed up this evening. It's been a long drive.'

'Where you from?'

'London.'

'What brings you down here then?' She busies herself moving various papers, food catalogues and bar towels around beside the till, presumably looking for some kind of register book.

'Actually my aunt died. She left me her cottage. I've come down here to sort out everything. There's no one else.'

I notice a frown flicker across her face as she retrieves a thick tatty black book from a shelf above the till and plucks a pen from behind her ear. The friendly air has gone for a moment and she looks almost distressed. I suppose it is not the happiest reason to be visiting though. She is probably used to people telling her they have come for the beaches or just for some peace and quiet.

'I'm sorry to hear that,' she says finally, passing me the book and the pen. 'Here pop your details in there for the room.'

'Thank you. Actually we weren't close.' I quickly scribble down my name and address before passing the book back. 'I don't even really remember her. Sort of feel guilty about that now. She obviously remembered me.'

'That's sometimes the way it goes,' she says simply. 'What else can I get you?'

I cast my eyes along the beer taps in front of me. Despite my earlier hankering for wine, I ask for a pint of Korev as I see it is a local beer. I figure I should do my best to fit in here. Any other order and I would probably be considered even greater an outsider than I feel now and I don't want to stand out any more than I already do being a new face. I just want to blend in, become anonymous again. Forget even who I am for a few days.

'Good choice,' she says as she pulls the pint and places it in front of me. It doesn't seem she is going to ask me any further questions about my aunt and I am sort of thankful. I don't know why. Maybe because I don't believe I'll have any answers and that makes me uncomfortable for some reason, like I'm some kind of fraud. I don't dwell on the feeling though and instead take a couple of sips of my beer. It is crisp and refreshing and the bubbles hit the back of my throat satisfyingly as I gulp it down.

'I'll get you the room key and I can show you up whenever you're ready. Menu is up on the board. Lamb stew is the best thing on there but it's all pretty good. Out of the pork chops though. I'm Sally by the way.'

'Elena,' I tell her, forgetting she probably just saw that was what I'd written in the book. My name seems to give her pause though but before I can get over my trepidation of getting into a conversation about my aunt and ask her if perhaps she knew her, she is distracted by something outside.

'Here look at these twats.' She points at a couple of men sitting on the outside window ledge, huddled over their phones and seemingly oblivious of the spitting rain. 'You know what they're doing don't you?' I shake my head. 'Getting my free Wi-Fi the cheeky gits,' she tells me with humour in her face. 'Watch this,' she beams and flips a switch behind the bar beside a sign stating "Grow your own dope; plant a man". We both watch as the men look at their phones for a few moments longer. One holds his up in the air staring hopefully at it before shrugging and saying something to his companion and then both reluctantly slope off into the night.

'Right, I'll get you that room key,' she says looking satisfied with herself before disappearing back out to what I presume is the kitchen. Somehow our interaction has made me feel more included and welcome. Sally's casual attitude with me is just what I need. I've had enough of people being careful how they talk to me, careful of what they say in case I might break.

Alone once more in a bar full of strangers however, I automatically take my own phone out of my bag so as not to feel so disconnected and to check if I have any messages from those same people who don't know how to act around me anymore. I see I have no signal at all here now the Wi-Fi is off and I hope that won't also be the case at the cottage, but then think perhaps I don't. Perhaps being totally cut off is exactly what I need. I put my phone away and notice I am no longer the centre of attention. Everyone has turned back to their own conversations or whatever ale they are drinking. Obviously I have not been found to be as interesting as hoped. I glance around at my fellow patrons, already feeling more relaxed with a drink in my hand.

A couple of young boys are playing pool. They are maybe late teens or early twenties. Their friend bangs a fifty pence piece on the edge of the pool table declaring he'll play the winner next. Their voices are a little more excited, a little louder than necessary and I can tell they've probably been here for a while and bet they won't be leaving till closing time.

Four men sit at a round table near to the boys. One is gesticulating wildly while his friends seem to be agreeing with whatever he is saying. One of them shakes his head, the other nods. The gesticulating man leans back in his chair and folds his arms over his ample stomach as if he has finished his proclamation and now is challenging anyone to take issue. I would not want to be the person who would disagree with whatever he said. He doesn't seem the type who would like someone with a different opinion to his own.

Then another man catches my attention. He sits hunched in the corner dressed all in black, black jeans, black shirt, black boots. Black hair hangs over his eyes. I'd say he was about my age but in the shadows it is hard to tell. He glances up at me, only a glance and yet there is something in his face which seems to penetrate me, to dive deep into me as if his eyes were fingers made of ice, reaching into my chest, grasping at my soul, finding it wanting. I look away quickly and although everything about him sends tremors through me I am also desperate to look back. When I do he has gone back to scribbling on a napkin, although exactly what I cannot see.

'London,' a gruff voice says. It is the man in the cap beside me. His companion must have left him for a moment.

'Um, yes.' I say because I'm not sure what else he's expecting.

'Been there once. Didn't care for it,' he sniffs, not making any eye contact with me. Now he decides to stare into his pint rather than staring at me the way he did when I walked in.

'Oh, I suppose it is quite different to here.'

'What part you live?'

'Kentish Town.'

'Yes. Don't know it.' He takes a swig of his beer. I wait for him to say something else before realising that's the end of our conversation and to be honest I'm too tired to try and keep it going so I also take a drink, daring to glance over at the man in the corner again and he looks back at me. This time I hold his gaze. There is something about him though I can't place what. Something familiar. Something unsettling.

'Here's your key. Have you decided what you want to eat?' I jump as the landlady, Sally, is suddenly beside me, then smile at her taking the key and hoping she hasn't noticed how frayed my nerves are.

'Lamb stew sounds good.'

'You want chips, jacket or dauphinoise potatoes with that?'

'Um, dauphinoise please.' I say distracted, considering whether I should ask her about the man staring at me but she carries on talking and for some reason I lose my nerve and the moment is lost.

'I said it right that time didn't I? Dauphinoise. They're always laughing at me in the kitchen 'cause I usually call them dolphin potatoes. Anyway I'll show you through to the restaurant side if you like. Bit more comfy to eat in there.' A cheer goes up as someone pots a black on the snooker table. 'And quiet,' she adds as she heads towards a door by the bar.

'Thank you.' I follow her, glancing back at the man in the corner one more time. He is still watching me. I tremble and hurry through the door pleased to be away from him. A few couples and a family are eating as Sally seats me at a small table and the atmosphere feels more relaxed in here. I decide I will go straight to my room after my meal. A part of me feels cowardly for not wanting to go back into the pub side but I have had enough of people staring, of accusatory looks. I'm away from all that now and I don't need anything to remind me of it.

Chapter 2

This morning I feel better. The sun is shining through the thin floral curtains of the guest room, splashing me with its warmth and making the room golden and glowing. It feels good to be away. Quiet with none of the noises I am used to outside my flat in Kentish Town. No sirens or lorries announcing that they are reversing. No buzzing engines of mopeds delivering things to neighbours or taxi doors slamming before they whisk people down into the city. I am now two hundred miles away from what happened.

I have a hearty breakfast cooked by Sally who then wants to know all about my life back in London. I do my best to avoid her questions and her insistence that I have an extra sausage and some bacon rashers as apparently I look like I could do with some meat on my bones. Instead I ask her about good places to visit in the area and what might be open at this time of year with so many places closed out of season. Together with her eagerness to tell me her recommendations, it is not hard to keep her from finding out too much about me as she is constantly distracted and flits from me to an elderly couple, who are also staying here, then disappears again, back into the kitchen or bar before there is time for anything much to be said. She is a tiny whirlwind, managing the place pretty much by herself apparently and seemingly doing a very good job.

As I finish my tea I look over to the couple at the other table. They introduced themselves as George and Cathy and visit here every year from Corby, Cathy told me proudly when they first sat down. George just managed a tentative hello and obviously was less keen to get into a conversation, something I could relate to. Sally had already whispered to me before they came down for breakfast that he's recently had a triple by-pass and I wonder if it was his sausage and bacon originally that Sally was offering to fatten me up with as I see him now looking forlornly at his bowl of porridge while Cathy, who seems twice as big in both size and personality, keeps a careful watch on him. Despite the obvious health issues a part of me envies them. It is easy to imagine other people's lives to be so much happier and less complicated than your own. Then I notice George attempting to liberally spread butter on his toast before Cathy snatches it away from him and scrapes off the excess before passing it back. Perhaps I don't envy George so much no matter how uncomplicated his life might seem. Though at least Cathy clearly cares about him, I think, and a little stab of envy returns though looking at George's expression I am not sure he sees it that way.

I say my goodbyes to Sally and promise I will be back again no doubt for another meal as the one last night was so good. As I swing my bags into the passenger seat of my car I look down the high street which shimmers still from rain we must have had in the night. There are barely any more people than when I drove through here yesterday. There is a small queue at the butchers and I see an elderly gentleman strolling down the road, paper under his arm and greeting a woman on the other side of the street being taken for a walk by a weimaraner. It is hardly a bustling metropolis and certainly a culture shock after the city but one which I could easily get used to and definitely one that is welcome at the moment. I jump in my car, swinging it round without issue in the deserted street and head back up the lane to the cottage.

As I pull up outside I see it looks much better in the daylight, quaint and certainly not the ominous and daunting project it had seemed last night. The wood in the window frames needs painting and some of the guttering has come loose but otherwise there doesn't seem much to be done on the outside, nothing immediately obvious anyway. For a moment I wish there was more; more of an excuse to not return to London.

I fumble in my bag and find the key I received in the solicitor's letter. The weathered oak door is heavy but opens easily. It reveals a small lounge with two large patterned rugs, all vines and flowers, spread across a wooden floor. A cream couch and two brown leather arm chairs are placed around a black wood burner which squats in the corner. Dark beams run the length of the ceiling and as I pull the green curtains back further to let in more light I see wisps of cobwebs hanging in a couple of the corners but nothing too bad. The place smells primarily of wood and incense though there is a faint musty smell from it being unoccupied for what I presume has been a couple of months though I don't know if my aunt was in hospital for any length of time before she died and again I feel a twinge of guilt for not knowing.

On one wall there is a large, antique looking mirror with silver gilt frame. I glance at my own tired reflection and see a face leering behind me, all twisted and green as if it has been made of roots. I turn to see that it is a mask hanging by the door. At first I recoil from it planning to take it down immediately but then I recognise it as the Green Man, a Pagan spirit and symbol of rebirth and not one to be feared. I have no idea how I know this. Probably from some book or movie or Irish pub back in London but he can stay there for now.

Above the fireplace there is a large painting of a woodland scene. I wonder if it is meant to be the woods opposite the cottage. Gnarled trees twist together to form an arch above a path covered with autumn leaves. Roots coil at its borders. More leaves, red and orange, drift down upon it from the crooked branches, shafts of golden sunlight shining upon them. As I go closer to the picture I see faces peering out of the trees. They are elfish with the suggestion of wings behind them, transparent and delicate but look again and they just seem to be more leaves floating to the ground, the faces just markings in the bark until you adjust your eyes once more and they reappear. In the distance there is a stag, white with huge antlers as twisted and unforgiving as the branches surrounding him. He is bathed in white light and amongst the trees various other woodland animals, badgers, rabbits and foxes are all turned away from the viewer and looking to the light shining in the distance and the path leading to it. The subject matter makes me feel it should be in a fairytale book somewhere and yet there is something very adult about the way it is depicted, something that suggests nothing of childhood innocence. I feel sure a child would have some sort of emotional reaction to it though and, had it been here when I was little, I would have been fascinated by it as indeed I am now but no memories spring to the surface and it makes me think it must be a recent addition and arrived after we had moved away.

On the mantelpiece there is a selection of crystals in a range of different colours and sizes though all small enough to be held in a hand. I recognise rose quartz and amethyst but the others I could not name. I pick one up and feel the weight of it in my hand. It is a brilliant blue and sparkles as the sunlight hits it. I stroke my finger across the rough stone and then up across the smooth crystals rising out of it. I wonder if she used them for healing or just enjoyed looking at them. I'd like to think just holding a crystal would make me feel better. Maybe I'll look up how to use them. Anything is worth a try.

I place the rock carefully back on the mantelpiece automatically making sure I have put it back just as I found it before remembering that all this is mine now and my aunt is no longer here to worry about whether some ornament has been moved. A part of me still feels she will come in, introduce herself and we'll sit and talk about old times. The realisation that she won't makes me feel suddenly very alone. Maybe you can miss someone you never really knew.

I look around for more signs of what she may have been like. There is a medium sized television set in the corner with some dead flowers beside it and a range of church candles of various sizes, some burnt down more than others, stand on the windowsills. A Buddha sits serenely by the fire place and a few books rest on the dark wooden coffee table. One is about meditation another about focussing energies to control your destiny. A third has a bookmark in it and I wonder if my aunt is still somewhere wishing she could have finished it. Signs of a life interrupted and it makes me sad. I pick up the book and flick through it; Moonchild by Aleister Crowley, an occultist in the early 1900s according to the dustsheet. Apparently it is a story about white magicians versus black magicians and something about the moon having influence over an unborn child. The magical practices depicted in it are meant to be based on Crowley's real life experiences. It goes with the territory. This area is known for its superstition and tales of witchcraft. I expect my aunt was quite a character and I wonder if she believed in all this stuff. I'd love to be able to ask her. I wish I had known her. I wish I could remember her.

    I put the book down and look at the rest of the room. There is a doorway beside the front door and beyond it I can see a small kitchen and a wooden staircase runs up the back wall of the lounge, curving round onto the upstairs landing. I head up it and find a small bathroom which just fits a tiny sink, toilet and old fashioned tub complete with brass feet and a large shower attachment on the taps. There are three bedrooms although one is no bigger than a closet. The first one I look in must have been my aunt's. The bed is large and old, maybe Victorian, with a carved wooden head board and looks freshly made up and I wonder if the solicitor got someone in to make sure the place was tidy for me. It matches a wardrobe, chest of drawers and a dressing table which is littered with perfume bottles and some half-used makeup. Beside the bottles a brush with a few light blonde hairs fading to grey still caught in it, waits to be used once more. I stare at it, once again trying to push away the feeling that I am trespassing here. That I have no business being in this person's bedroom, looking at their personal things and at any minute I will be caught snooping. As I think this I get a flash of an image of not looking down on the dressing table as I am now, but looking up. Standing on tip toe, my small child's hand is reaching for a particularly ornate perfume bottle and I can hear laughter but as quickly as it came, the image is gone and once more I am left guessing if it were a real memory or my imagination. Just me wondering if I did come in here as a child, looking for makeup and playing make belief, trying to be especially quiet so I wouldn't get caught before I'd had a chance to sample the spoils of the dressing table. I stand for a moment, staring at the bottles, waiting for them to perhaps jar my memory once more but they do not so instead I go to the closet. There are still dresses hanging in it. They look very bohemian, all patterned and flowing and I'm getting the overall impression that my aunt was a bit of a hippy though still cannot picture her wearing any of them. I close the closet door and look around some more. A small window looks out over the garden. I go over to it and lever it open, welcoming the fresh air. The turquoise and white dream catcher hanging on the frame jostles in the breeze, feathers fluttering. I look out across the garden and over the tops of the trees in the woods and realise that I can just about see the coast beyond, a small triangle of blue glistens, darker and richer in contrast with the pale sky. I take a deep breath and can taste the ocean. I can hear wind chimes tinkling somewhere below me and can imagine for a moment that I don't have a care in the world. It is definitely good to be away from everything.

    The second room I go into is about the same size as the main bedroom but much lighter with none of the dark wood furniture. Instead all is white and the single bed has a pretty white counterpane and frilly pillows with a large soft bear dutifully keeping watch upon them. I go over to him and hug him to me wondering if he was once mine. He doesn't tell me anything though so I place him back on the bed. There is a white chest below the window and I find that it is full of old toys. I can see tea sets mingled with Barbie dolls and princess costumes complete with tiaras and wands and wonder if going through this will jolt some memories. That can wait for another day though. The shelf beside the bed also has toys upon it, some of which are porcelain dolls and I don't mind admitting they're not my favourite thing in the world. They rank somewhere up there with clowns. I feel a pang of guilt in case my aunt was very fond of them but they will have to go.

It is when I am coming back down the stairs that the memory hits me.

I am being dragged down these stairs and I am screaming.

'Take the back way out. They won't come that way.' I see my aunt, she is wearing a long yellow dress which floats around her as she runs to the stairs, her blonde hair tumbles across her shoulders and her normally calm and happy face is twisted in anxiety. She is afraid but I know it is not so much a fear of those who are approaching the house but a fear of me.

'They are wrong about her you know,' my mother says as I struggle but her grip on my arm is hurting me and grows tighter the more I try and get away. 'And so are you.'

My aunt looks at me and I don't like the look. I am as afraid of her as she is of me. Of what she knows or thinks she knows.

'Just go!' she whispers.

I blink. What was that? Surely not a real memory. Surely something conjured from an overly eager mind trying to recollect a lost childhood. Whatever it was it leaves my heart pounding and I feel my skin prickle with a cold sweat. I stagger through the lounge and into the kitchen and lean against the sink, flipping the faucet and splashing my face but the water makes me want to gasp. I don't want it on me. I slam my hand on the tap to stop the flow, turning my back on the sink and breathing heavily, feeling like each breath is a struggle.

What is happening to me? Another panic attack. That is all it is. The past months have just been too hard. I shut my eyes and focus on the solid ground beneath my feet and nothing else. I feel it supporting me and my heart beat begins to slow. I can just about breathe normally again when there is a knock at the door.

'Hello, hello, can I come in? Anyone around?'

I walk from the kitchen and see a man poking his head around the front door and I realise I must have left it open. It takes me a moment but then I recognise him as the person who had been sat in the corner of the pub the night before and I feel my recently calmed heart skip once more but this time the anxiety doesn't take hold. No longer in the shadows of the little bar I can see his features more clearly. His face is long and angular and his nose is a little crooked and looks like it may have been broken several times but it does not make him unattractive. His large blue eyes are deep and piercing and lined with dark lashes but it is the warmth in them which is the most striking thing. His clothes are still all black and something tells me there is very little colour in his wardrobe. A wallet chain loops at his hip and he wears a thick leather cuff bracelet on one wrist and I have my suspicions that he may be a bit of an emo but his smile is huge and radiant and he does not seem sinister as he did last night. Still I am wary of him and of the reason he is now standing on my doorstep.

'Hi,' I say.

'Hi,' he says and then just looks at me as if surprised there was anyone here and he hadn't prepared anything to actually say if there was.

'Can I help you?' I prompt before the silence gets any more awkward.

'Ah, yes, sorry,' he nods seemingly snapping out of whatever dream he was just in, running his fingers through shaggy black hair causing it to look even more unkempt. 'Actually that was what I was going to ask you. You're new around here aren't you?'

'Yes.'

'So I overheard you had come to fix this place up on your own and that there was no one else to help you.'

'Wait, how did you know..,' I start to say. I know I hadn't mentioned any address, not even to Sally.

'It's a small village. Everyone knows everyone around here. Your aunt's name was Carol wasn't it? She seemed alright.' His words come out quickly and there is a slight nervousness about him which betrays his easy smile and stance. 'I knew she had no one around here to leave her estate to. I wondered if she still had family elsewhere.' He takes a few steps inside and involuntarily I step back and I must look uncertain because he stops and looks a little hurt. 'Sorry, I shouldn't have presumed. I just thought I'd offer my help if you need it. This village can be quite a hostile place to newcomers sometimes and last night you looked like you could do with a friend.' He hesitates. 'I'll go.'

'No, no don't. I'm sorry. I'm just a bit on edge lately. It's very kind of you to offer. Thank you.'

'No problem,' he holds his hand out to shake mine. 'Name's Will by the way.'

'Elena.'

Something changes in his face as I say my name and take his hand. He stares at me for a moment and the sadness in his eyes makes me want to run to him. To tell him that it is all OK though what is OK or not OK, I have no idea. As quickly as it came the moment has passed. He swallows, shaking his head a little as if waking from a trance.

'Um so this is going to sound weird but did we meet in London years ago?' he asks.

'Ah no, I don't think so, but I meet a lot of people so...'

'You would have been at university?'

I shake my head.

'Sorry.'

'I must have been mistaken,' he says but he looks confused, shaken even. 'So tell me how I can help. What are you going to do with the place?' he asks as if all is normal, his voice almost too up beat and I still detect a tremor in it.

'Um, I don't know yet. Look it's really kind of you to offer but honestly there isn't much to be done. I don't want to cause you any bother.'

'It would be no bother. I do landscape gardening normally so this time of year things are pretty quiet. Not that I'm looking for a job,' he adds quickly. There is a desperation about him that I don't understand and suddenly I just want him gone. In my experience nobody does anything for nothing and I am not ready for new people in my life right now, any people in my life. He steps towards me and something in his eyes changes again. It is as if he is trying to work something out about me, like there is something he can't quite believe.

'Really, I don't want to waste your time.'

'I'm sorry, I've intruded.' I see his hand rise and I think that he is going to reach out as if to touch me but then he quickly pulls back. 'If you change your mind though here's my number.' Slightly flustered, he rummages through his pockets finding a pen and an old receipt and scribbling his number onto it. 'If you change your mind.' He hands me the paper, his blue eyes staring earnestly at me, into me, just as they did last night. The intensity unnerves me and I know that I will not be using the number now in my hand.

'Thank you,' I say and he nods, a gentle but unsure smile playing on his lips before I watch him leave. He turns back once as if to say something but then is gone. I close the door and go into the kitchen, dumping the receipt in the bin as I pass it.

Chapter 3

By nightfall I feel more settled. I have spent the day dusting and cleaning and had the satisfaction of feeling that I have been productive today. I managed to lose myself in the chores making my mind blissfully numb, not allowing it to wander to its usual dark places, to regret the past and fear the future.

The local charity shop was very grateful for all of my aunt's clothes. I carefully boxed them, looking at some of the older dresses to see if they jogged any memories of her. None did. Then I came across a yellow one, long and flowing just like in the vision I had earlier. I felt myself tremble as I cradled it for a second remembering what I thought I must have imagined, what could not possibly have been really the past, before burying it in the box under a load of old jumpers and skirts not wanting to consider its similarity to what I saw for any longer than I already had.

After that I opened all the windows and got rid of the musty smell and let the sun shine in which went a long way in making the place feel alive again. I moved all my things into her little bedroom and I am beginning to feel less of an intruder than I did this morning. I even managed to work out how to use the Aga and cook myself a half decent risotto for dinner rather than going back down to the *Lady of the Lake*, which had seemed the only viable option at one point. I can almost pretend that this is home now and I can be anyone I want to be here, leave the past behind me and pretend it never happened. At least that is what I tell myself.

Now I sit with a glass of red wine and a blanket around me, curled up in the chair in front of the wood burner it has only taken me three attempts to light, and start to read my aunt's unfinished book.

The wind is picking up again outside. It howls around the house and I hear the trees groan in its wake. I look up from my book shivering a little, still to get used to the unique noises every house has. Despite liking being away from all that happened, I suddenly feel nostalgic for the sound of traffic and sirens back in Kentish Town, the feeling that there are other lives going on nearby, the familiar soundtrack of my evenings and I wrap the fleecy blanket a little more tightly around me.

The wind silences as quickly as it had started. Now the only noise is the crackle and spit of the fire and the creak of leather as I shift in my chair. And yet there is something about the surrounding silence. It feels as if someone or something is holding its breath. I glance around the room. Everything is in its place. The Buddha still guards the fireplace, the green man grins down from the wall by the door and although I cannot make them out from here, I am sure the elves are still safely hidden amongst the trees of the painting, the firelight warming their faces as it dances across them. I am just not used to being this far out in the country. I take a sip of wine and go back to reading my book realising I must have read the same paragraph four times now.

That is when the tapping starts. It is soft at first and methodical, coming from the window just behind me. I guess some branch outside. I will have to look in the morning. I am too tired and cosy to be bothered to get up and find out the cause right now so I try to ignore it and get back to reading but the tapping seems to get louder, incessant. I am still sure it is just the wind and will stop in a moment but my normally rational mind which can usually block out annoying noises, as is sometimes necessary at work and indeed living in a flat, starts to imagine things. I feel as if someone is just outside, face pressed against the window knowing I am in here, waiting for me to respond. Their fingernails playing on the cold glass, desperate to get in and however hard I try and get lost in my book I find myself constantly looking up to the window where the noise is coming from.

The tapping gets louder still, more menacing. I stare at the window, at the heavy green curtain hiding whatever is making the noise from sight, and try to summon the courage to see what is waiting for me outside but just as I am about to leave the safety of my chair the noise changes and a dull thud quakes through the room as if someone has lost patience with their gentle knocking and punched the window hard in frustration.

All is silence once more.

I wait for the tingling feeling of electricity to seep from my chest and down out through my fingers allowing me to breathe again but do not take my eyes off the window for a couple of minutes, sure that the noise will return. It does not. It was just the wind, nothing more, slamming against the house. No one is trying to get in. No one is angry that I am ignoring their knocking. I am simply spooking myself. I open my book once more. This time I manage to finally finish the paragraph and even start on the next page before my concentration is once again interrupted.

Tap tap tap.

This is ridiculous. Putting my book down, I go to the window. Maybe I can open it and see what branch is making all the noise and snap it off right now without having to go outside and my mind will stop conjuring up fantastical images as if I were five years old rather than a grown woman with a degree and a mortgage. And yet all my rationality doesn't stop my heart pounding and my throat closing as I pull back the curtain.

The tapping stops. There is nothing there.

I fling the window open. There is no tree close to it and the night is still, the moon bathing the garden and woods beyond, turning everything to blue and shadow.

It must have been a bird, maybe an owl trying to get in. Do owls do that? I have no idea. There aren't too many owls near my flat in London. I close the window, swishing the curtain back across it and go back to my chair, wrapping the blanket around me once more.

I wait for the noise to return but it does not. The evening is still again and the warmth of the fire caresses me. As I finish the final drops of my wine the pages of the book begin to darken. I strain to keep my eyes open, just to the end of the chapter then I will retire to bed, leaving the fire to slowly die…

I am on the roof again. The air is freezing and there are flecks of snow in the sky, no doubt exciting the shoppers far below who are hoping it may be a white Christmas in four days time. On a clear day you can see almost all the city from here, now nearly all is cloaked in white mist. I can just see the lights from the top of the Shard in the distance, the colours shifting from red to green today and then a twinkling golden muted in the fog. I often come up here. It gives me a chance to breathe, away from the clamour of the city, to be alone with my thoughts even just for a few minutes. This was one place in London I could feel solitary but this time I am not alone. He has followed me up here. I heard the door of the stairwell close and now I can hear his footsteps, slow and methodical, tap tap tap as he comes towards me. The cigarette drops from my fingers down to the street below. It drifts impossibly slowly as if time itself is freezing in the mist. I watch wisps of ash trail from it as it spirals away from me into oblivion and I turn to face my tormentor. He is a silhouette in the fog but I know that it is him and as I push myself up against the barrier behind me, feeling the concrete beneath my hands, I imagine it as a tomb, cold and enduring, ancient with blackened weeds tangled around it decaying without just as that which is enclosed decays within. The heavy lid worn with fading epitaph keeping the dead secure so that they cannot rise, they cannot return, they must stay dead. Locked away and buried and just like me they are powerless to escape.

I wake. My heart is pounding and the tapping against the window has resumed. That was what triggered my mind to remember the footsteps, to remember that day.

I get out of the chair and go to the window again, flinging back the curtain.

It is his face that stares back at me, the man from my dream, ruined and bloodless and full of hate and revenge.

I scream.

This time I really wake. I take deep breaths trying to convince myself that I am OK. That it was all just a dream. He is gone now. He can't hurt me.

The book slips from my lap and falls to the floor, jarring me back to reality, the slip of paper my aunt had been using as a bookmark flung from its pages, losing my place. I pick up the book and then look on the floor for the bookmark. Seeing it lying under the table, I grab it but then

I realise that what I have found is not the same paper I thought I had been using. I hold it up and turn it over.

It is the receipt with Will's number on I had thrown away earlier today.

Chapter 4

I awake feeling tired. My head is heavy although my sleep, thankfully, had been dreamless after my nightmare, maybe thanks to the little dream catcher still hanging on the bedroom window frame, I think, smiling at the thought it could be that easy to rid myself of my troubled nights. No harm in leaving it there though just in case it does work.

I go downstairs and make myself some coffee and find some cereal in one of the cupboards. As I pour it into a bowl I notice Will's number which I had put on the kitchen counter before going to bed and trying to forget about strange noises and bad dreams. I don't know why I didn't just throw it away again like I already thought I had. Maybe my subconscious knows more than I do and he would be good to have around. I haven't decided yet. It was strange it had made its way into my book but I have not been thinking exactly clearly lately. It spooked me last night. Today it seems more troubling that my mind is that scattered I don't know what I've thrown away and what I have not.

After breakfast I step outside and the day feels unseasonably warm. There is a soft breeze but nothing more and the only sounds are the tweeting of birds and my aunt's wind chimes, my wind chimes.

I look to the woods beyond my garden and the path running into them and feel even more certain they are the same woods as in the painting. If so I wonder what the light which all the animals are looking at might represent and whether venturing into the trees may offer a clue. I could use a walk to clear my head so I decide to find out. Pulling on my boots, I stride out, taking in the fresh air. It is just what I need. I take deep breaths imagining they are cleansing me, breathing out all the stress, all the badness and replacing it with purity and light just like all the books tell me to. It is the most peaceful I have felt for months.

As my feet crunch through the detritus a gust of wind hisses through the trees but I hear no other sound apart from my own footsteps. Not even birds now, and certainly no distant traffic, nothing. It is calm and solitude and bliss. I can see why someone would be inspired to paint here.

The path forks and I decide to take the left track which has a small wooden post beside it stating that it leads to the beach. The ocean seems a perfect place to lose myself and I am not disappointed. I follow the track beside a twisting and babbling brook for about a mile or so until I come out of the trees to where the cliff falls away about thirty feet. There is a spit of sand below me but otherwise it is all black rocks and crashing waves. I look out to the horizon. There are no ships in the distance, just the blue of the ocean glistening like the crystal back at the cottage on the mantelpiece, stretching out to distant shores. Maybe that is why it is so calming. It promises new lands, new worlds, perhaps even a new life should you venture across it, and at the same time its vastness makes everything feel less significant. In time all our problems just like ourselves will be gone, faded to memory and dust but the ocean will endure and I wonder how many others over the years have stood, looking out from this spot just as I am doing now.

Closer to the rocks I see a dark object before it dives out of sight and I smile thinking it must have been a seal. I wait a few moments, staring out at the blue and hoping that I will see it resurface but it does not and I wonder if it was my mind playing tricks on me and it was just a rock or piece of driftwood, the waves breaking over it and giving the illusion that it was something of more interest. Still there will be plenty of time to seal spot I am certain. There is a steep path leading down to the beach with a railing which looks to have seen better days. I consider taking it but I am unsure whether the tide is going in or out and it wouldn't take long for that patch of sand to be lost completely. I decide I will find out the tide times and come back another day. Feeling sand between my toes, even what I am sure will be quite cold sand, seems very appealing to me right now. I spend a few more moments watching the spray flung from the waves as they seem to climb over each other in their race to get to shore, roaring as they reach their destination and leaping up the cliffs before being swept back out again. Then after taking one more deep breath of the salty air I head back into the woods.

 On the way back I realise just how much more relaxed and refreshed I feel for the first in a long time. And also I realise something else. I realise I feel like I am home. There is a familiarity about these woods of the kind I was expecting to feel at the cottage but did not. I look across at the stony banks of the river, at the pebbles sparkling and shiny as the water moves over them glittering in the mid-morning light. At the bright emerald green moss lining the roots which reach down the banks curling and curving over one another and it feels as though this is how this place must have been for centuries and certainly in the times of King Arthur when people still believed in magic and faeries and the spirits of the forest. And as I think this I see that some people still do believe in such things. Someone has stacked stones neatly on top of each other on the bank, a rickety tower of somebody's hopes and wishes and thanks for those dreams which have already come true. A cairn, the old Celtic word slips into my mind. Of course it may be for mundane reasons such as marking a trail but somehow I think not, especially when I see the bright pink ribbon tied to one of the branches above it. Somehow I know that the ribbon is also meant to represent a wish and a memory drifts into my mind like a caress.

I am maybe six and on this very bank I am sure. I am looking down at my feet which are clad in pink shiny wellies with little green dots on them which I recall being very fond of. My aunt is beside me but nothing like the anxious and frightened woman I thought I had remembered on the stairs yesterday, if that indeed was a real memory. This time she is a vision of calm. Her blonde hair is like the sunlight and her skirt flows around her, green as the moss at her feet. I look up at her and I am fascinated by the cluster of necklaces she wears; one a white crystal on a leather string, another a pentagram with blue gems at each point and another, a tiny silver lady, her arms held aloft; "the goddess" my aunt had explained once, and I was entranced by the trinket. I imagined the land in which the goddess might dwell but also strangely believed that perhaps my aunt herself was the goddess, come to teach me all that she knows. The pendants dangle and clack together as she bends to find another pebble as smooth and flat as the first she has laid down beside the river.

'Now you find one Elena and think of a wish as you place it on the pile and then whenever we pass here we can see our pile of wishes and remember to give thanks for them if they have happened or to focus on them if they are still to come.'

I smile now at the memory, for this is one which I am sure is real and I find that I am trembling slightly because of it. There is something strange and intimate about remembering a relationship with someone I had forgotten. I really did love my aunt, idolised her even and in recalling this some of the guilt I feel about her leaving me everything is diminished but only to be replaced by guilt that I could have forgotten her at all. It is certainly the earliest recollection of my childhood I have ever had though and somehow it makes me feel grounded. I have a past now whereas before I did not and I had felt as if I was floating in the ether with nothing to cling to.

'Thank you,' I whisper to the pile of rocks and to my aunt, wondering if she is listening somewhere, wondering maybe if it was she who had placed the rocks and ribbon I am looking at now. For I feel certain if spirits do exist she would be amongst the trees and in the woodland air, watching over me just like the goddess I used to imagine she was, pleased that I had found her cairn and that she has helped me to remember a tiny piece of my past at least. 'I'm sorry I forgot you, I'm sorry I abandoned you.'

The rest of my walk along the river is uneventful and it is only when I am nearly back to where the path forks that the chimes start.

At first I think it is my imagination. I stop, the sound still ringing in my ears. It sounded like a tiny bell echoing through the woods. I look up into the trees that loom over me like mournful creatures, their arms outstretched, the knots and twists in the bark looking like silent screams, nothing like the friendly faces of the painting back at the cottage. I listen closely to hear the noise again, but all is silent once more so I continue to walk but then another chime does ring out, this one a different tone. And a few seconds later, another.

It is as if someone is holding a music box mechanism and turning it very slowly. I start walking faster though I find myself inexplicably heading further into the trees down the right hand fork I had ignored earlier, rather than running back to the safety of the cottage, drawn by the sound despite every note striking terror through me. I do not know why the sound fills me with such a sense of dread except for the fact it is so unnatural in these surroundings. I have always been curious however. The old saying of curiosity killed the cat is not lost on me. It has proven very true on one occasion. I just like to think I have eight lives left.

As I head deeper into the woods I feel as if I am getting closer to the source of the sound and yet the chimes never get any louder. I think I can piece together a tune now though. Perhaps a child's nursery rhyme, but which one I cannot remember. The trees begin to thin out as the path becomes muddier and I find that I have come to the edge of a small lake.

A green film covers the still waters, shimmering like an oil slick and there is a faint stale odour of mould and of things which are rotting beneath the surface. There is no foliage surrounding the lake, the branches of trees hanging over it are naked of leaves and I can see no buds promising the coming of spring. No fallen leaves disturb the waters either, no grass goes to the edge of it. There is only dirt and decay and death.

And yet I step closer only now realising that the chimes have stopped. I stare down into the waters. A bubble breaks on the surface. Not all is dead in this place.

Something lurks beneath the slime. Another bubble silently emerges dispersing as it hits the air.

And the chimes begin again.

Except this time they are not so much chimes but more like the toll of a bell, mournful and deep but still with a scratchy, metallic sound of a music box and still slowly peeling out the distorted tune.

I glance around. Could it be that there is a church near here? Is that what I heard before? The church in the village is not that far away. Did I just imagine it to be chimes?

But this does not sound like a church bell either. This sounds like nothing holy.

Another bubble breaks on the surface of the water, larger than the other two.

I step back, losing my balance as my foot hits something, probably a fallen branch, but I manage to stay standing, not even glancing back to see exactly what it was which nearly toppled me as I cannot take my eyes from the lake. For some reason I am transfixed by it. Two more bubbles come to the surface. I do not want to see what is disturbing the water. Something tells me it would be very bad to see it. And yet my feet are not moving. They are fixed to the spot now as I watch the bubbles coming faster and, as a gust of wind swishes through the trees and finally I am able to look away, look up at the swaying branches, someone inhales beside my ear. Not a gasp but a long, slow rattling breath which gurgles in their throat.

I turn, a scream catching in my own throat but there is no-one there, though now the spell has broken and my feet are no longer helpless. Now I can run from the lake and whatever lies beneath its surface.

I stumble back down the path ignoring the thorns and branches catching on my clothes, my heart thundering in my ears and I am pleased for that as it drums out the memory of what I just heard.

    I dare to glance back, just to see how far from the lake I am, to convince myself that there is nothing there, and that is when I can see the black dome in the water, small like the very top of a child's head, tendrils of what might be hair spreading around it like ink or poison oozing from a sea creature.

    I know it is my imagination. I know it and yet as I run my mind tortures me into thinking someone or something is just behind me. That they have clawed their way out of the water and across the muddy banks and are now scuttling to catch up with me. My neck and spine tingle as if I can feel their stagnant breath upon me and I have visions of a twisted and decayed arm reaching out almost touching me, the gnarled fingers stretching with nails torn and blackened trying to grasp me and pull me back to the depths of the lake. As I think this a branch, for I am sure that is all it can really be, tangles in my hair but any rationalisation that I have merely got caught on a tree is overridden by fear and instead of stopping I plunge forward, ripping the tangled strands from my head.

    I do not look back again until I have reached the edge of the woods and I can see my cottage in the distance. Only then do I dare to stop running. My legs are heavy and aching with the sudden exertion and I draw ragged breaths as I steel myself to look back. The path I have just run twists innocently away from me, the air around it still, with a few flecks of pollen floating in the beams of sunlight filtering through the trees. There is no trace of the terror I just felt fleeing along it. There is nothing there.

    I take a deep breath feeling foolish now for letting my imagination run away with me and walk as calmly as I can across the road, resisting the urge to jog the last few steps to the safety of my home.

That is when I notice a man is standing outside my front door and despite knowing he will likely think I am crazy with leaves and twigs tangled in my hair and sweat pouring down my face I am very happy he is there. I wonder what he wants. Whatever it is I will welcome the distraction.

Chapter 5

'Morning,' he calls to me as I approach. He looks smart, in his fifties perhaps with thick grey hair and wearing a tweed jacket. His trousers look to have been carefully pressed and his shoes buffed. I suddenly feel self conscious in my sweats and wellies and wonder what happened to people being more casual down here. He is not especially tall although his stature makes him appear so and gives him a domineering presence. His eyebrows are also thick though slightly darker than his hair and covering the top half of his eyes so it is hard to read his expression or what he must be thinking as I come towards him most likely looking like a hedge witch. I notice how much my hand is shaking as I open my gate and hope that he does not.

'Morning,' I call back, managing my best smile before I take a deep breath and try and compose myself. It will be a hard enough job trying to convince people I fit in here I have decided, without the added challenge of having to explain that I spooked myself on a simple walk in the woods by imagining bells ringing and the forms of children emerging from lakes.

'I was wondering if you'd seen a young girl, a child,' his voice booms, authoritative with no trace of a West Country accent and the words jolt me from my thoughts. I feel as if he has read my mind, as if he is tormenting me but I know that cannot be the case.

'No,' I reply and yet I feel I can hear a lie in my voice and I wonder if he can sense it too. But there is no lie. I walked alone this morning. I certainly saw no other living thing. 'Why?' I manage, sweeping a clump of tangled hair from my face.

'A child has gone missing from the village, Grace. She is only five. Mother went to wake her this morning and she wasn't in her room. Think she climbed out of the window.'

'Oh my god, her mother must be frantic. If there's anything I can do.'

'Just keep a look out. I'm sure she will be fine. Not much trouble she can get into around these parts. Seems she got sent to bed early last night for some misdemeanour or another. Her mother checked on her around 10 O'clock and she was sound asleep. I reckon she slipped out of bed just after to teach her mum a lesson. She's a wilful one I can tell you.'

'Oh, has she done this kind of thing before then?'

'No, but you know how at that age being sent to bed early can be the end of the world and must mean your parents hate you. Running away seems like the good and only option. We've all done it at some time when we were kids I am sure.'

I nod and smile sympathetically though I have no idea whether I have or not.

'Took her favourite grey bunny with her,' he continues like he is reading off a report. 'I'm certain she can't have got far. She'll be home before tea no doubt when she gets hungry and realises life with her mum and dad isn't so bad after all, but be nice to find her sooner. That's why I and a few others are asking around, helping out the police.' He preens a little as he says this, puffing out his chest. 'Besides no telling what outsiders might be about in the village,' he adds.

I don't know whether the term "outsiders" is aimed at me or not but I feel slighted by it anyway, like I am being accused of something. It is not the time to be over sensitive though.

'I'll keep my eyes peeled. If I see anything I'll let you know,' I say sincerely keeping my voice light so as not to show I even considered his words might be testing me.

'Much obliged.' He nods at me and walks to the gate but turns back before he opens it. 'Trouble in the woods this morning?'

'What?'

He taps his neck gesturing for me to do the same. I do and my fingers come back with blood on them. I wipe at my neck again and can feel a tiny scratch where a thorn must have caught me.

'I tripped and fell,' I say quickly. 'No real harm done, there are some nasty brambles in those woods though.'

He nods but doesn't seem convinced and looks as if he is going to say something else but changes his mind at the last minute. Instead he stares at me for a moment, looking troubled then shakes his head and continues through the gate. I don't know whether to feel puzzled or offended. I decide not to feel either. This is a tiny village. People are so used to their own company and the usual handful of familiar faces I suppose it is only to be expected that they become distrustful of anybody new, worried that a stranger will upset the fragile balance of the community.

I head inside, grateful to shut the door and have a barrier between me and the woods once more despite reassuring myself that nothing sinister could really, possibly dwell in them. I still find myself peering through the little window in my front door though, watching the man walk back down the lane before staring back at the path into the trees which had looked so inviting an hour or so ago and a sudden dread comes over me. And I pray the missing child has not wandered where I did, has not stumbled across the lake. And even though I know that what just happened out there was a manifestation of my overly stressed mind, that just like the man said, there is little trouble to be found around here, I feel very afraid for the little girl. Very afraid indeed.

***

I am on the roof again looking at the snow specked sky of London. I am thinking of my coat still hanging on the back of my chair at my desk. Why did I leave it down there?

Because I had to get out. I had to think.

I take a long drag on my cigarette. To think I had almost given up. I blow the smoke out into the darkening sky where it mixes with the fog and disappears from sight. I wish I could follow it. Dissipate into nothingness.

I hear the door of the stairwell and I know now that when I turn it will be him. I have had this dream enough to know exactly what happens next. To know my mind is replaying a memory and I am not living it at this moment. That there is nothing I can do to change what happens next and even if I could change the dream it would not change the reality.

I turn to see him, a faceless figure in the darkness. I am helpless and cannot alter my actions and would I anyway if I could? The figure approaches but he is not as imposing as usual. His build is slighter and as he emerges from the fog I see his eyes are blue but not cold, not soulless as they are on all the other nights I have had this dream. He reaches out to me and now I see that it is Will, a man I have only met once and yet I start to cry, my feelings for him overwhelming and I don't want to hurt him. I never wanted to hurt him. He is…

'This is not you,' he says and I wake.

It takes me a moment to get orientated. It is still night and I think I am back in my flat in London but then I remember I am not. I can see lights outside however, not the usual pitch black. I get out of bed and look out of the window. Shafts of light dance and pierce through the blackness. I see them flickering in the woods.

They are looking for her. The lost girl still has not been found. I pray they will not go further into the woods than necessary. I pray they will not find her in there for if they do she will not be the same girl she once was.

I shake my head. I don't even know what my own thoughts mean anymore. What am I even thinking could have happened to her? I don't know what is happening to me. All I know is that this fear won't go away. Fear of the past, fear of the future, fear of everything around me.

Fear of myself.

I close the curtains and block out the night before returning to bed but I can still see the lights and I stare at the window wondering what is happening beyond it for an eternity before I finally allow myself to fall back to sleep.

Chapter 6

The day brings sunshine despite the weather forecast predicting more heavy rain. The air is fresh and crisp and as I breathe it in I feel equally fresh, the strangeness of yesterday forgotten. Nothing is in those woods. I know that. I wonder if they have found the girl yet though. I am sure that they will and that she will be fine. I look into the woods as I collect the post from the little box on my gate. They look inviting again like they did yesterday before my walk. Snowdrops have finally managed to burst their way through the hardened winter soil and now sway in the breeze at the borders and I can hear birds again. The scene is idyllic. They told me before I came here I would likely have good and bad days. Yesterday was just one of the bad ones.

As I turn back to the house I jump as I see a figure by the door. This time it is Will. I do not know how he got there without my seeing him. I take it there is another gate I haven't yet discovered. I've not really looked properly around the back of the house yet. There seems to be more a thin strip of overgrown scrubland than a garden behind it and not something I really want to deal with at this point and besides there has been enough to keep me busy inside. Of course Will, being a gardener, might be seeing a whole lot of possibility. Whatever he says about not looking for a job I don't believe him. He'd be foolish not to try and drum up some new business especially if work is slow as he said.

'Hi there,' he waves as I walk to him, his head on one side and a crooked smile. His hair still falls slightly over his face as the wind catches it. He brushes it away but it drops right back and eyes which look quietly amused about something peer at me from underneath it. I didn't notice before quite how attractive he was and then I remember my dream from last night. How I felt about him in it and I feel my cheeks flush.

'Hi,' I say nervously, going to my door.

'So you never called.'

'I didn't know it was mandatory.' I rest my hand on the doorknob not wanting to go inside just yet. If I do I shall feel like I have to invite him in and I am still uncertain whether that is something I want to happen.

He shrugs and there is a shyness about him as he looks down at his feet then back up at me with those eyes.

'I guess it isn't, but you looked like you could use a friend so I hoped you would. Like I said sometimes friends aren't that easy to find around here.'

'Not anywhere,' I half smile but hope I haven't invited any unwanted questions.

Or maybe I do want him to ask. Maybe I want to confide in someone that I may have killed a person and that guilt eats me up every day but it is made worse by the thought that I am not sorry they are dead. A part of me is truly happy that they are.

'Have you lived here all your life?' I say. Keep the conversation on him. It is the safest way.

'Yes.' The answer hangs in the air. A simple little word and yet there is a weight about it and his eyes bore into me as if he has answered so much more.

'Do you remember me?' The question is out before I realise what I am saying.

'Yes.'

We stare at each other and I would love to say that I understand why, that unspoken thoughts fly between us but it is as if we are silently communicating in a language I don't speak and he is waiting for me to remember him, like we have some kind of history. But how could we? I must have been only seven when I left here. If I'd had friends, close friends, I'd remember them wouldn't I? But then why would I when I don't even remember myself.

Then the world tilts, the cottage, the woods as they are now, all fall away and I see us both as children. We are in this very garden but it must be late spring and the sun is warm and drenching everything in a golden afternoon light. A gust of wind whispers through the trees sending pink blossom floating down all around us. We laugh as it drifts down, softly landing before swirling up again, the wind sweeping it into an eddy and causing the petals to settle on our clothes and on our hair. And I watch Will, his arms outstretched as he twirls in the soft pink rain and although his hair is much lighter than it is now and I can see the face of a seven year old, the eyes are still the same, deep and blue and framed with the darkest of lashes. And even though I can't be more than about six years old in this memory I remember the feelings I had for him and how I was imagining this to be our wedding day; the petals our confetti, the wind our loved ones casting it over us as we begin our new lives together forever. And I remember how I wanted to tell him this but I dared not but I knew that one day I would. Maybe on our real wedding day I would remind him of this moment and he would admit that he was thinking the same.

Why have I never remembered this before? And suddenly this memory seems more real than any since then. My life in London, graduating, getting the job in the city, relationships, holidays, moving into my flat, evenings out, evenings in, birthdays, Christmases, heartbreaks, my mother's funeral, it all seems like a dream. Like it happened to someone else. I never stopped being six years old and I never stopped being in love with William Malone.

Did he ever tell me his surname?

'William Malone?' I ask tentatively, shaking at the force of the memory still and he smiles at me confirming the memory wasn't just a fantasy, wasn't just my brain trying to fill in the blanks the way it always has before.

'I remember you,' I say, excited that finally I seem to be getting my past back. 'And I haven't been able to remember much of anything from my childhood before but you, you were here with me in this garden. There was blossom everywhere and some freak wind making it swirl around us.' I look around at the now barren grass imagining it as it once was. 'It was really magical,' I murmur wistfully.

'It was.' I hear a crack in his voice as he confirms it was a moment he has not forgotten either and I look back at him but unlike me he is not glancing around his surroundings thinking of how they once were. Instead his gaze is still fixed on me but his eyes have so much pain in them that I almost have to look away. And there is something else beneath the pain, there is fear.

'Why didn't you say something the other day when you came over?' I ask trying to keep my voice steady under the intensity of his stare.

'I just wanted to make sure it was really you.'

And the fear in his eyes dissipates but the intensity does not and for a second I forget to breathe.

The moment is broken by a scream. Actually more of a screech, angry and ripping its way out of the woods.

'What the hell!' I jump. Will catches my arm as I take a step towards the woods, ready to investigate whatever such a noise could have been.

'Don't go in there,' he tells me and there is a tremor in his voice.

'But you heard that didn't you?'

'It was probably just a fox or something.' What he is saying sounds plausible and yet the fear in his eyes is back as he looks towards the trees, betraying his words.

'That may be so but what if it wasn't. Haven't you heard about the little girl who went missing, what if it was her and she's in trouble?'

'Elena!' he warns.

'Will, I have to see what that was.' I shake his grip off irritated that he should be trying to stop me and a little confused as to why he is. Then I notice his face. He looks…broken.

'Don't,' he says quietly. I want to ask him what's wrong. What is he scared I might find? Has he seen something lurking out there in the lake as well? Has he heard strange bells and gasps which have no obvious explanation? But there is no time. If someone is in trouble I have to see if I can help. I can't stand by and not act again. I can't have any more on my conscience.

And so I leave him and run to the woods where, only yesterday, I was so convinced I would never return. I try and think where the sound would have come from. All is deathly silence now as it was yesterday before the chimes started, and my heart is pounding but I am not as afraid as I was before. My worry for the safety of someone else over rides my overactive imagination. Besides I am not expecting to come across any real danger. If the girl has wandered into the woods and fallen or broken her ankle she needs someone to come and discover her. So why does something feel wrong about the idea that she is all that I am searching for, just a little girl in despair.

Because last night they would have found her.

Because the scream I just heard was not that of a child. I am not even entirely sure it was human.

I start to jog down the same path I took yesterday except this time I take the right fork not once thinking to try the coastal path for I know that is not the way to whatever made that noise. Looking this way and that I try to see any signs of movement or life but all is still, tranquil, but rather than feel calm or relieved about that, I feel frustrated. I run faster, my searching for whatever called out becoming more frantic. What am I doing? I feel desperate and lost and I don't know if I am trying to save the girl right now or to save myself though exactly what from I cannot tell. And then I find myself back at the lake. It spreads out before me still, desolate and baron. I feel as if it is a living thing, challenging me to come nearer. I stop and stare at it, pushing yesterday's imaginings out of my mind. There is not as much as a ripple on the stagnant water now. No sign of anything about to break the surface as there was yesterday, or did I imagine that too? I go closer to it, jogging around the edge wondering if what I heard lies beyond the waters where the trees become dense once more and the path is overgrown and uninviting with thorns and brambles twisting over it. I am speculating on how much further into these woods I can go when my foot catches on something.

I fall heavily, damp mud seeping into my clothes and leaves fly up into my mouth dry like the husks of moths. I spit out the dust and take that moment where you realise you are on the ground so fast you don't even remember falling and I roll over to see what it was that put me there.

And that is when I see the hand, small and curled, half buried in the mud but beneath the dirt I can still make out the greenish white of the skin, the sickly look of flesh that is putrefying. It is a child's hand and the fingernails are black and ragged where they have clawed at the bank and I know if I take hold of it I will haul the missing girl out of the lake. I turn away feeling the bile rising in my mouth and scramble back from the water. I cannot summon enough breath to scream, I cannot do anything.

And then Will is there. I didn't know he had followed me. The light is different though than it was a second ago. The sun is higher as if I blinked a whole two hours away. Did I pass out? I'm sure I didn't.

He rushes to me, taking hold of my arm as I try to sit up. 'Elena, thank god I found you. You just ran off. You've been gone hours.'

What?

I can't think about whether I passed out or not right now.

'Will,' I try and keep my voice steady. 'Will, behind you; the little girl. The little girl who went missing.'

Will glances behind him, looking out across the lake to the trees beyond. He turns back to me.

'What are you talking about?

'Her hand Will,' I say feeling the tears piercing my eyes as I try and hold them back. 'She's in the lake, she must have fallen in there and tried to claw her way out. She must have...' My voice fails me as I think about what must have happened.

Will gets up and looks down at the muddy banks.

'Elena, there's nothing there.'

'There is! It's a child's hand Will! Look in the mud!' I wave my hand in the direction of the lake, not wanting to look at what I'm trying to point at. Not wanting to see the pallid flesh again, the nails betraying how desperate she must have been as her fingers sunk through the sludge, scratching against stones which must have given false hope of a purchase among the soft dirt around them before they too broke loose and sunk with her into the fetid waters.

Will paces up and down the bank kicking at the mud and I wish he wouldn't do that. He needs to stop doing that. He shakes his head.

'Elena, I promise you. There is nothing here.'

'There is Will!' I cry. 'I saw it, just a second ago!'

Though just a second ago it was morning and Will just said I'd been gone for hours.

'Elena I think you've had a fall, bumped your head pretty bad.'

'I didn't even hit my head,' I protest. 'I know what I saw!'

Will looks at me for a second, forehead creased in concern and I know he is trying to work out if he is more worried whether what I am saying is true or about my seeing things that I only think are, and I don't know what else to say to make him believe me. Finally he nods.

'Ok, Ok. Look we'll get the authorities to check it out. Could be the poor kid sunk into the lake. It wouldn't be the first time.'

'It wouldn't?'

He shakes his head looking deep into the waters.

'No.'

The word is whispered and chills me more than it should. More than hearing this place has a grim history, more than imagining others' plight as they try and cling to the unforgiving mud which slips through their fingers as the lake swallows them down. And I can feel the burn of yellow stagnant liquid filling my lungs to the point I start to choke and fully expect to see water fall from my mouth but it does not.

Will rushes to my side once more, putting his arm around me and helping me to my feet. 'Come on, let's get you warm and dry and we'll tell the police what you saw. They'll have to dredge the lake. At this point I'm sure they were thinking of doing it anyway what with it being three days since the girl went missing.'

'Three days, I didn't realise. The man I spoke to yesterday said she'd only disappeared the night before. Monday night.'

Will frowns at me. 'Elena today is Thursday. They've been searching for her for days.'

Chapter 7

The questioning has gone on for hours. How many times can I tell them what I saw? That, no, I didn't know the little girl; yes I think I heard a scream but I'm not sure; yes I'm on some medication but nothing to make me hallucinate that I tripped on some poor child's hand; mild antidepressants, that is all. Despite the repetition making me wonder if they were trying to catch me out, waiting for my story to change in some tiny way, the police were nice enough on the surface. They brought me tea and store brand biscuits and put their understanding, compassionate faces on but I could still tell they were one step away from accusations. The hushed talks outside the room, the fake smiles when they came back in. By now they would have got my file from somewhere no doubt, learnt that this wasn't my first time to be interrogated. Before was much worse though. There were no smiles then, just shouting and assumptions of guilt but this still feels it could turn that way at any second.

Now I wait in the bare grey room for the inspector who has been quizzing me the most to return. My chair seems to grow harder with each passing minute as I sit hunched over a Formica table, my fingers wrapped around a chipped mug of tea which is already growing cold. I try to come to terms with what I just saw and of the days which I have apparently lost but which I did not mention to the police. It is enough trying to get them to believe that I am telling the truth without giving them any other reason to question my credibility. I stare at the mug in my hands, at its off-white colour and the faded blue logo on the side of some company who no doubt supplies paper towels or locks to cells or who the hell knows what that police stations use which comes with tatty merchandise as some sort of thank you. I wonder how many have drunk from this mug before. How many witnesses, how many victims, how many criminals? Their shaky hands clasped around the vessel just like mine are now, trying to focus on what has just happened, what they've just seen, what they've just heard. What they've just done. That first moment when the numbness, the shock, the disbelief wears off and the pain sinks in and steps are taken to cope with it. To decide what to do next.

The door opens.

'You are free to go Miss Reynolds.'

The inspector stands in the doorway though does not come right in as if not wanting to commit himself to my company for any longer than necessary. He reminds me of an old school teacher I used to have, his face weary from being subjected to stories and excuses on a daily basis and an impatient air about him as if he is just waiting for the next lie to come along, almost hoping for it.

'Have you found her?'

He studies me for a second and I can see him picking his words.

'No.'

Quite a simple word to take so long to pick.

'Well did you dredge the lake? She has to be down there.'

'We've searched the area and she wasn't. There was nothing to be found in that lake Miss Reynolds.'

It takes me a moment to process this. I look at the mug again, at Celeste written in big blue letters. Locks or paper towels? The thought wafts into my mind stupid and trivial amongst the whir of unanswered questions.

'I don't understand. I know what I saw. She can't have gone far.' I sound desperate and vaguely realise the wrongness of that. Do I really hope that they will find the little girl at the bottom of the lake just to prove me right? Shouldn't it be a relief that they have not and that she has not died in such a horrible way? That there is still a possibility that she is out there alive somewhere and it was all just my imagination after all.

'Miss Reynolds, there was no girl in that lake or indeed anywhere around it. Now I don't want to speak out of turn but I am aware of what happened to you a few months ago, of your past. Maybe you need to arrange someone to talk to. We have leaflets here.'

'I don't need leaflets!' I'm yelling and wish I wasn't. Everything I say now will make me seem even more unstable and what is worse is that I am starting to believe the hype. 'I'm sorry,' I put down the mug. 'I'm sorry to have wasted your time.'

I get up from the table, the chair screeching against the floor and echoing off the bare walls as I push it back and I walk past the policeman unable to look at him.

As I walk through the station towards the door I see a couple. The woman is sobbing, greasy hair scraped back into a pony tail while a man with bloodshot eyes and a few days growth of stubble holds on to her. They look up at me and watch as I walk to the door. The woman's eyes are full of hate and I feel as if it is only the fact that the man is holding onto her which is keeping her from running over and attacking me.

'Don't,' I hear him whisper to her and I know then that these are the girl's parents. I have just put them through even more unnecessary grief. They have reason to hate me perhaps then.

But I know what I saw.

Chapter 8

I am back in my bedroom looking out of the window at the woods beyond. My hands are still shaking and I feel nauseous, the events of the day and resulting questioning playing over and over in my mind and instead of my own face reflected in the glass, all I can see is that of the girl's mother, etched with anguish and the want to hurt me as much as I have just unwittingly hurt her.

And there is nothing I can do to change that. Nothing I can do to make it better other than hope I really did imagine what I saw. And then where does that leave me? Where does it leave the missing girl? No good can come of anything that has happened today.

I push the image of the mother's face from my mind and try to focus past my own reflection to the trees outside once more. There are no lights tonight spearing through the branches as there were last night, or was it two nights ago? I really have no idea now.

I need something to calm me down. I look at the pot of antidepressants beside the bed. I have tried not to take any since I got here hoping that the change of scenery would heal me rather than chemicals giving me the illusion that I was getting better. However after my first encounter with the lake I thought that it wouldn't harm to take one just to help me sleep. I am beginning to think that was a bad idea. Maybe I shouldn't be skipping medication and then going back to it. The tablets are only mild though. I was assured I was unlikely to have any side effects but maybe they are the reason I have been imagining things lately and the police were right to ask me if I was on any prescription drugs.

But I didn't imagine the child's hand, of that I am certain however much it would be easier if I could make myself believe that I had. But then was that any more real than the figure I saw emerging from the lake, the chimes that I heard, the wretched gasp behind me before I ran certain that someone or something was chasing me through the woods? All things that could not possibly have been anything more than my imagination.

No.

I decide I shall not turn to the pills again but I do remember there is a packet of cigarettes in my coat pocket and that's when it hits me that I haven't smoked since I got here. Maybe it is all the clean air. In fact I can't remember the last time I did smoke. I want to give up, maybe I should keep this as a promising start and not reach for the packet but this doesn't seem a good time to quit. Besides if I've gone at least three days before…

Four days, I remind myself. *Four days.* S*omewhere you lost a day.*

But whatever, if I've done it before I can do it again just not today. I go to my jacket and the slightly crushed box nestles deep in the pocket as hoped. I flip open the lid. It is almost full. Be a shame to waste a packet if I gave up now anyway.

I open the window and the cold air hits me, chilling me even further though the physical chill is better than the emotional one I am feeling. More easy to control and understand. I pull a cigarette out and then the lighter I've tucked next to it. Popping the cigarette between my dry lips I try and light it, sucking the air in deeply, desperately like some kind of junkie eager for the resultant hit.

And cough, my lungs burning in protest. I drop the cigarette. Has four days not smoking made me like a beginner again? Surely not. But I have no want to feel any more nauseous than I do already. I pick the cigarette up quickly making sure it hasn't singed the wooden floor. A bit but nothing that will show, hopefully it will look like a knot in the wood. I stump it out on the outside sill and shut the window before putting the lighter and cigarette back in the packet. Later I will come back for it no doubt.

As I try and push the lighter down into the box something is stopping it. I shake the packet, jostling the cigarettes around a bit before trying again but something is still keeping it from fitting back in. I upturn the box shaking the contents from it so that they scatter across the window sill and a neatly folded piece of paper drops down onto them. I pick it up expecting it to be some competition or the usual warning that I am going to die of lung cancer or some other horrendous condition but as I open it I see my writing. Some note though I can't remember making it or why I would have put anything in with the cigarettes. As I begin to read a chill runs through me and I forget to breathe.

I am Elena Reynolds, something is happening to me. I am not myself. I am at my childhood home but do not know how I got here. Found out Nathan is dead. I was a suspect. Is that why I've blocked out everything since the roof? But that was almost two months ago. Online paper said today's date is Wednesday February 19th. Want to go outside, buy an actual paper, talk to people to find out more but this headache is excruciating. It is hurting to even write this.

My hands feel clammy as I carefully put the note down. Wednesday the 19th. Yesterday. The day I have lost. What is happening to me?

Does this mean there was really no hand, no chimes in the wood, none of it? Am I actually losing my mind? I wrote a note to myself to suggest just that as if I knew I would forget the lost day. The version I am now seems in better shape than the one I was yesterday, I have only lost a day, the other me seems to have lost months, but still. How many more blackouts can I have, and why now? Why not before? Surely this cannot be caused by taking one antidepressant? It is not like I haven't been on them since Christmas.

The walls feel as though they are coming down around me but the thought of going to my therapist about this terrifies me. Just imagining what she might tell me, that she could confirm my worst fears and that I am in fact seriously mentally ill makes me feel as if all the air has been sucked out of the room and I am falling with nothing to grab hold of to stop me. Am I schizophrenic? Is this the first sign that my life is over? From now on will it all be medication and white coats and doing jigsaw puzzles in some soulless room with others who lost who they were? Who are just lost?

I close my eyes, desperately trying to recall writing this. I picture myself sitting with the cigarettes, scribbling on the piece of paper which I realise is from my aunt's pad by her phone. I must have been in the lounge. I must have got out of bed and gone downstairs and...

And what? Forgotten the entire last two months of my life?

Just like I forgot the first seven years of it?

I don't want to deal with this right now. Apart from all the nausea of what has just happened, I feel fine, I know what I saw. I know what is real and what is not. I scoop up the cigarettes and put them back in the packet with the lighter. I take one last look at the note and then screw it up and go to throw it in the bin but then stop myself. I open it out again, smoothing it with my fingers and reading it once more. This has to be something to do with the medication. It has to. Nothing more. If I lose more days then I'll worry but until then it was just some weird glitch caused by the antidepressants or maybe just sleep walking. I've heard it can happen. People can do house work and everything all while dreaming. I always thought it sounded like a good trick to have. Maybe I was that exhausted I slept a day but my body didn't know it or something. I always return to that time on the roof in my dreams, maybe a part of me was still in that time when I wrote the note, hovering somewhere between the reality of now and the dreams of the past. I don't know. I can't think about this right now and I can't be on my own.

This time I really do throw the note away and I find Will's number.

Chapter 9

'You sounded upset on the phone. Was the questioning OK? I was going to wait for you but the police told me I should go home and actually I wanted to go out to the lake. See what they found.'

Will stands on the doorstep, the darkness behind him absolute. I cannot even make out the silhouette of the woods against the night sky as the moon must be hidden behind heavy clouds. The cold sweeps into my warm cottage like a breaking wave and I tense as it washes over me. Winter has managed to get one last hold on the land, not giving up its place to spring just yet. Its cruel icy fingers digging into all that hoped warmth and new life were finally here after the long cold months.

'They found nothing,' I admit, the words feeling hard in my throat and tasting of the confusion and embarrassment that I feel saying them. I open the door wider so he can walk past me and notice that he smells of spices, of wood smoke and of cinnamon.

He nods, 'I know.'

'You should have seen the way her parents looked at me Will.' I shut the door and turn to him. 'It was as if I'd taken their little girl. As if I'd drowned her.'

'You can't think like that. You know what you thought you saw.'

'What I thought I saw?' I am instantly irritated. 'Will I didn't imagine it!' I protest realising I am shouting at him and instantly regretting it. It is not him I am angry with. I am not sure who I am angry with. The policemen for failing me? For failing the little girl and her parents by not finding anything? Or am I angry at myself for not being in control of my emotions, of not being certain of anything right now? And with that thought the anger just goes and leaves only despair. 'I don't think I imagined it,' I mutter. 'But I just don't know anymore.'

And the tears come. I feel stupid crying in front of this relative stranger I haven't seen since I was seven but I have no choice. It feels as if all the walls I have spent the last months, perhaps years, building up are now all crumbling and the despair, guilt, even relief though I cannot tell for what, are all rushing out. Maybe this is what I need. I talked to my therapist after what happened of course, but I was always holding back. Always aware that the real reason she was sat there was because I was paying her. I just need someone who actually cares and doesn't need fifty pounds an hour to listen or to pretend to. Someone who I don't feel is silently judging me, sitting there watching as I judge myself.

I feel Will wrap his arms around me and I sink into him, burying my face against his neck, his soft hair, his spicy scent. It envelopes me and I feel safe.

'You didn't deserve any of this,' he whispers. 'You never did.'

I look up at him, blinking away my tears. What does he mean by I never did? What does he know about me? I feel myself tense. Has he looked me up online? Has he found some obscure article about what happened back in London and put two and two together, realising I am the Elena Reynolds they will have been talking about? Does he know what I am running from? Somehow I don't think this is about that though. Something tells me he is talking about a much earlier time.

'What do you mean?'

His brow furrows and I see his jaw tighten as he searches my face and I can see hurt and I can see anger but I have no idea for what. 'Nothing,' he says finally. 'Just that you are a good person Elena, don't let anyone make you believe otherwise.'

I glance at the stairs and think of the memory I had of being dragged down them. Of feeling hunted and of the fear in my aunt's face as she told my mother and I to just go. Did that really happen?

'Do you know why I left here? Did I ever say goodbye to you?

'No,' his voice cracks. 'You never said goodbye. You never got the chance.' His fingers gently stroke my face as he sweeps a strand of hair back behind my ear. Again there is something unspoken in his eyes. He is telling me something but I am too ignorant to understand. Why doesn't he get that I just don't remember. What is he waiting for me to remember?

I am about to ask him why. Why would I have just left and never said goodbye? Why didn't I get the chance? What happened all those years ago that meant I left so quickly? Why did we never come back here? Did my mother and I really have to flee? And if so, from what? What could have driven us from this village and caused us never to return? But before I can ask anything, a thunderous knock at the door breaks our embrace.

I wipe my eyes quickly sniffing back my unshed tears and letting Will go to the door. Three men are there, one of them is the man who told me about the missing girl, his frown making his eyebrows hide even more of his eyes than they did the other day. I learnt from the policeman earlier that his name is Geoffrey. Seems he is quite an esteemed member of the community and on the council though I got the impression that the police tolerate more than respect him. The others I do not recognise but they both look to be around retirement age and have an air of authority about them. One is thin and bony with a grey beard closely clipped to his pointed chin making me think of Punch from Punch and Judy if the character had been washed of all colour and turned to grey. The other is a barrel of a man. He stands with his legs apart and leaning slightly back as if he wants to display his huge stomach, like he is proud of it. His eyes are beady and brown and he holds his head high, looking down his nose at Will which makes his eyes look even smaller. He holds his mouth as if he has just eaten something bitter. There is an arrogance about all of them and the demeanour of those who believe they know best though who never travel far enough out of their comfort zone physically or metaphorically to learn any different.

'Will,' Punch says, surprised. 'What are you doing here?'

'What's it to you?'

'We don't want any trouble. We just want to speak to Miss Reynolds,' the barrel cuts in.

Will looks as if he is about to protest but I walk forward before he does. I know that he knows I'm upset but there is no need for hostility.

'Will it's OK,' I touch his arm, 'I'm up to talking.' Reluctantly he moves away from the doorway and I face the three men. 'Do you want to come in?' I offer. The cold comes off them in swathes and I do not want to stand with this door open any longer than needed.

'That won't be necessary Miss Reynolds. What we have to say is brief,' Geoffrey states, the words harsh and clipped as if he resents wasting breath on having to speak to me at all.

'OK,' I'm a little taken aback by his tone. 'Go on then.'

'We'd like you to go back to London. Tomorrow preferably. As you seem to have befriended Will here I'm sure he will gladly finish any business you have with the house. You can put it on the market, probably fetch a fair price and you never have to show your face here again.'

'What?' I am flabbergasted, 'What is this? I don't understand.'

'There is nothing to understand Miss Reynolds, just know that we don't want you here,' Punch adds simply as if he were explaining it to a child.

Will is immediately by my side holding my arms as if I am going to lunge at these men though I don't think it will be me who will chase them off my property.

'She's not going anywhere,' he spits, 'and you have no right to come here and try and make her do anything.'

'Our village was peaceful before she came here Will, just like it was after she left. Now she isn't even back a day and a child goes missing. We were willing to let it slide but after today…' The barrel rocks on his feet as he speaks as if he feels it gives his words more weight.

'After today what?' I cry, 'You think I had something to do with a child going missing? That I just then wasted police time pretending I'd found something? I don't believe this. This is some kind of joke surely?'

'This isn't open for discussion Miss Reynolds. We want you gone tomorrow, the next day by the latest,' Geoffrey states.

'And if I don't go?'

'Like I said, this isn't open for discussion.'

'Right now it's you who needs to go.' Will pushes me behind him and stands nose to nose with Geoffrey who remains unmoved. Will is no real threat to the man and certainly not with his two goons flanking him. They are older men but I am under no illusion that they can't handle themselves.

'This doesn't concern you Will.'

'Yes it does. And I said you need to go.'

'We'll go,' Geoffrey steps back, 'but she needs to as well.' He points a neatly manicured finger at me and I recoil a little from it and from the pure hate in his eyes which flashes as he glances in my direction before looking back at Will. 'Perhaps you were too young to remember everything Will but we all do. She never should have come back.'

'I said go!' Will yells. The men back away calmly and nod their assent like they don't want any trouble but I am certain that they will keep their word. They will be back if I don't do as they say though I am not sure how they can force me out. Right now that is not the main thing which is worrying me though. Have my fears really just been confirmed? Were my mother and I chased from this place all those years ago? It is becoming more and more difficult to convince myself that what I envisioned on the stairs when I first got here wasn't a real memory. That happened. It must have. And yet...

Will watches them walk down the path, Geoffrey holding the gate for the other two to pass through as if they have all the time in the world and have just conducted a routine business meeting. Certainly not like men who feel under any sort of threat from Will. It is only when they climb back into their Land Rover and start the engine that

Will shuts the door. He turns to look at me and his face is as drawn and as exhausted looking as I feel.

'You Ok?' he asks. I shake my head, watching as the headlamps of the Land Rover light up the night outside as it passes the window and then all is darkness once more.

'What did they mean by you were too young to remember Will? Too young to remember what? What is it that they think I did? That's so bad they'd treat me like this?'

'Nothing, you did nothing,' he takes hold of my shoulders making me focus on him rather than the blackness outside, rather than the thoughts of what I might have done. 'They're old men, senile, bored; threatened by anything that hasn't lived and breathed every second in this village. I don't know.'

'They weren't that old.' I glance back at the door as if I can still see them standing there, their accusatory expressions, their assuredness that they were doing the right thing telling me to leave. There was certainly nothing senile about any one of them. They seemed to know exactly what they were doing and what they wanted.

'Doesn't matter. This is a small village where any new face is unwelcome.'

But it doesn't seem to be my being a new face that is the problem. The problem is whatever happened to me as a child and probably the reason those years are blank. What could be so terrible that I would have blocked it out? Worse, what is so terrible and also my fault that a village wants to block me out too.

'Will I'm sorry, sorry for dragging you into all this.'

'You have nothing to be sorry about Elena and I'm here for you. I want you to know that. Not everyone in this village is as short sighted and ignorant as those men.' He holds my gaze, his eyes smouldering, still full of anger but there is something else in them too, perhaps sincerity, determination that he will protect me but perhaps something else. And another emotion wells up inside me in reaction to it, bubbling and aching and needing but I am unwilling to deal with it so I push it down convincing myself that what I really need right now is to be on my own. There is just too much to process and I realise that if Will does know something, if he does remember what may have happened that could cause seemingly respectable men to come to my house and threaten me, he is not going to tell me what it is, at least not at this moment when I am so vulnerable. And to be honest, right now, I don't want to know. I feel like the slightest thing could tip me over the edge though my imagination of what may have happened all those years ago may be worse than the reality. I somehow doubt it though, especially as I can't actually begin to imagine what a six or a seven year old child could possibly do to cause grown men to hate and distrust her years later.

I just need to rest. Maybe tomorrow I can face more but right now I am exhausted from the day's events and from the tears and I feel my head throbbing. I feel bad saying this to Will after bringing him out here but I think he'll understand. I think he understands much more than I do.

'You need some rest,' he tells me as if proving this, his eyes full of concern. I nod. 'I can stay, if you want. I can sleep on the couch. Be here should you need me.'

I think of my sleep walking concerns and shake my head.

'No, its fine. I'll be fine.'

'You're sure,'

I manage a half smile and nod, too tired to say any more words.

'Ok,' he says quietly, gently squeezing my shoulders reassuringly and a part of me does not want him to let go, does not want him to leave me here alone but I say nothing and he goes to the door once again, opening it and letting in the biting wind. It wasn't as strong a moment ago, now a gust catches my hair and seems to cut through my flesh to the very bone. I shiver. He turns to look at me.

'I'm happy you're home Elena,' he says before disappearing into the night.

Chapter 10

    I fall asleep as soon as my head hits the pillow but again my night is not peaceful. This time my dreams place me in the spare bedroom, sat on the floor cross legged for I am a child again. The porcelain dolls watch over me from their shelf but I am not afraid of them even though a part of me knows that usually they would make me uneasy. Right now though I have no reason to feel any trepidation for them and I even find that they are quite beautiful with their lacy bonnets and old fashioned dresses but they are not what hold my fascination at this moment. My hands are clasped around a silver music box and I carefully wind the large key on its base before opening it and watching the figures of two little children turn inside. Music rings out sounding as if it is being made by tiny magical bells, haunting with a slight scratching noise as the mechanism rolls and the key clicks around, winding down, slowing into silence before I wind it again and watch the children dance once more. I place the box neatly on the floor in front of me, entranced by it, entranced thinking about who gave it to me. And the curtains behind me billow into the room, white and flowing like the sheets of a morgue. Dry leaves sweep through the window, settling on the carpet and the box and my hands but they do not bother me. Then the blossom floats through the window but it too is as dry and dead as the leaves but still I think of it as confetti although now browned and shrivelled with age. And now I think of the curtains as the veil of a ghost bride equally aged and shrivelled but unaware that she is no more and still stumbling and running, desperate to find her lost groom. The image of her fades away, the music box soothing everything into calm but then I hear footsteps and these do trouble me. They are running up the stairs, echoing on the wood and creaking on the floorboards of the landing and I know they are those of a child as they are light and quick. I close the music box. For some reason I do not want anyone to know I have it. I do not want anyone to take it from me so I push it beneath the bed but I am sure it will have already been heard. Something is stopping it from going as far under the bed as I feel it should, something soft, spongy, maybe a blanket. The room is darker now as if a great cloud has descended over it and as I sit in the half light the footsteps stop outside the door. The knob rattles and begins to turn and the door slowly opens but I cannot see who is there yet. I turn back, frantically trying to push the music box further under the bed and in doing so my fingers brush against whatever is stopping it. Not a blanket. Nothing soft like clothes or bags or things I would expect to find hidden there. It is clammy, like mouldering cheese left out on a summer day, and I can visualise the moisture forming on it and I can imagine the buzzing of the flies around it growing louder and louder until they become more than imagined and it feels as if they are filling my head. But what I am touching does not feel like some forgotten foodstuff, instead it has the feeling of flesh but with no heat of life within it. And I want to scream but I daren't because I know now that the door is fully open behind me and something far worse than whatever is beneath the bed is waiting for me in the shadows. I can hear its breathing and I can feel its hate and although I don't want to turn to see who is there, I do and…

I am an adult once more and I am on the roof and the figure approaches me but again it is not the same as in the countless nights I have suffered this dream. Again the man approaching is Will.

And then it isn't. Then Will is beside me and I am looking at Nathan striding towards me as usual. Looking at the man whose death I feel responsible for. He is nearly upon me and I know in this moment that he is deciding whether to throw me from this roof or beat me to a pulp and leave me up here for the cold to finish off and there is nowhere I can escape. Nowhere I can hide. He is holding a hammer. Not a big one. It's not like we have easy access to such things in our finance office but some refurbishment is being done on one of the levels you have to pass to get up here. Several of my colleagues have complained of the noise on some days. I wonder if he stopped to see what he could find. I wonder if he explained to the builders what he might need a hammer for. The hammer is all I can focus on and then I hear Will's voice, whispering in my ear.

'Welcome home.'

And I want to cry and the breaths I am taking are hurting like fire in my lungs and my heart feels as though it has been pierced with pure hurt and loss and I turn to Will.

'You betrayed me. Why did you betray me?'

I wake.

Gulping in fresh air I feel relief as my lungs are no longer burning. My mouth is as dry as if it were filled with ash though and so I decide to head to the kitchen for some water. As I pass the guest bedroom I see that the door is ajar. I can't remember leaving it that way so I go to close it but as I do a gust of wind howls around the house, ripping my hand from the knob and flinging the door open further.

I step back in shock before realising I must have left the window open in there when I was trying to get some fresh air into the house earlier. It only occurs to me when I am in the room that this would normally slam the door shut rather than rip it open. In any case the window is open, the white fine curtains billowing around it.

I hurry over to it, slamming down the sash and sweeping the curtains across to block out the horrible night. As I turn I notice a dark shape in the middle of the floor. I am sure it was not there a second ago. I would have stepped on it surely as I went to the window. I cannot make out what it is and for a awful moment I wonder if a rat has got in, for it looks to be about the size and with the glow from the landing light I can see what looks like fur. I wish I had turned on the light switch by the door when I came in so I could now better see what it is. I don't want to walk past it again in case it is a rat and it will run at me. I tell myself to not be so silly but still I walk quickly past it, almost leaping to the light switch, holding my breath as I flick it on terrified of what it may reveal.

In the middle of the floor is a grey soft toy rabbit. It looks to have been well loved but is now covered with mud which is matted in its fur. I walk over to it wondering if it had been on one of the shelves and I hadn't noticed, only to be dislodged by the wind, maybe by the curtain flying out from the open window and knocking it to the ground. But there are no shelves near the centre of the room and the wind has been bad but not that bad.

As I approach it I can see an eye hangs loose and I don't want to touch it as it looks so dirty but I do, picking it carefully up between my thumb and index finger and it is only then that I realise it is soaked through and reeks of the lake in the woods.

I drop it and run from the room, shutting the door behind me, this time making sure it is closed properly. I back away across the landing, staring at the doorknob, expecting it to turn at any second and I think of what the man had told me about the missing little girl when she had first disappeared. That she had taken her grey bunny with her. I have no doubt that that is what is now in my guest bedroom. Has she climbed in through my window? Is she hiding in that room? No, nobody was just in there I am sure of that but still I cannot bring myself to go back in to find out.

I do not go back to sleep.

It is morning before I venture back into the room.

The toy is still there. It makes me feel sick to look at it. I walk quickly past it and sweep up the counterpane of the single bed. Nothing is under there. Then I open the small wardrobe, my heart slamming in my chest as I do so but I have to put my mind at rest. A few old coats hang inside but nothing more, certainly no cowering child hiding from whatever. I walk back across the room not looking at the toy again. I can't deal with it right now. I go back out onto the landing, slam the door shut behind me and wonder if this is all happening on purpose. Some people in the village want me gone. How far would they go to make me flee back to London? Suddenly I am very determined that I am not going anywhere and if one of those ridiculous old men actually climbed up to my guest bedroom to put that thing in there I shall find out who it was and make them pay. Though what am I meant to do now? Call the police and tell them I've had an intruder?

'Did they take anything?' I imagine them asking.

'No but they left a wet soft bunny in the middle of my guest bedroom.'

I start to laugh and although it is verging on hysteria it actually feels good. No doubt those men will be coming back before long expecting me to be all packed up and ready to leave and when they do I shall throw that wretched thing at them and make sure it is as wet and as muddy as when they planted it in my house. Let them know that I am on to them and they'll have to do a lot more to frighten me back to London than leaving soft toys lying around. I begin to wonder if the child is even still missing. Perhaps she has been found but they are still using her as an excuse to see me go for some reason. What kind of mind would do that though? What kind of person would think it was OK to use a child in distress as some kind of tool? A sick one I think and I am better than anyone who would sink that low, whatever I may or may not have done in the past. And whatever happened to me as a child, I was six maybe seven. Just how much harm could a child that age really do? It is ridiculous to even worry about it anymore.

I go to the fridge and realise that I am out of milk. A walk into the village will do me good and buying some groceries will let anyone who may be concerned know that I have no intention of going anywhere just yet.

I sweep my hair up into a pony tail and put on my Hunter wellies before striding outside. The wind has dropped now completely and although it is overcast I can see a break in the clouds and it looks like it may turn out to be a nice day. Maybe I'll invite Will to the cottage tonight. Cook him a meal; a thank you for putting up with my craziness. I am sure that wasn't what he was signing up for when he offered to be my friend. And if he wants to tell me what happened to me when I was a child, if he even knows, he can. If he doesn't that's OK too. I'm not going to care anymore.

As I get further down my lane I can see blue and orange flashing lights and hear the sounds of cranes and engines whirring. I go towards them but a man in a high visibility jacket stops me.

'Sorry Miss, can't go down there yet.'

'Why, what's happened?'

'Car accident. Happened last night by the looks of it. Only found them a few hours ago though. Seems everyone was holed up, what with the storm and that, so no one came across them for a good while.'

'Oh god, are they going to be OK?'

'Fraid not miss. No escaping what happened here. Act of God and all that I suppose though act of the devil seems more appropriate.'

I crane my neck around to see what has happened thinking of how many times I have hated looky-loos at accident sites. Rubberneckers I call them and yet this is exactly what I am doing now but I can't stop myself. I can see a Land Rover. My stomach lurches as I also see a body bag beside it. The crane is trying to lift up a tree which has fallen onto the car yet the roof does not seem to have crumpled terribly. Surprising considering the size of the tree and if I hadn't been told differently I would imagine there could be survivors. Then I notice what has kept the roof from caving more. Not the fact that it is a well built vehicle but the fact that branches have pierced it stopping the main bulk of the tree from falling as much as it could have. There is a screech as the branches start to move and scrape out of the metal and that is when I see the dark figure of the vehicle's driver moving too. And for a moment I think maybe he is alive and almost call out to tell someone but then I realise it is not only the roof which has been pierced but also his head and neck and now he too is being pulled by the crane.

'Whoa whoa whoa,' a man shouts, signalling to the somewhat oblivious person in the crane's cab. 'What are you doing? Not yet! Not yet!'

The crane operator manoeuvres some kind of lever and the tree is slowly replaced, the driver of the stricken vehicle flopping back to his original position.

'For Christ's sake,' the man who had shouted for him to stop utters angrily and that is enough for me. My rule to not rubber-neck has served me well in the past. I should have kept to it.

'How long till it's cleared?' I ask, trying to keep the tremor from my voice. My day-glo friend looks equally traumatised.

'Couple of hours I reckon. Sorry. As you can see it's a mess.'

'No problem,' I say, giving him a sympathetic smile. I wouldn't want to have to stand here while those other two bodies are extracted from the car. I do not envy his job at all.

I make myself some green tea when I get back. Don't need milk for that. And try and forget what I just saw though I think it will stay very fresh in my mind for a while. I sip the hot tea and try and imagine it cleansing my mind as well as my system.

The day which I thought would turn out nice has turned to grey and I see the first spots of rain appearing on my windows. There is something cosy about it, though I am sure the poor men at the accident site will not be feeling that way.

I find myself pushing the image of the impaled figure in the crushed car from my mind once more and take another gulp of tea, watching as the rain drops come faster and larger, streaming across my window, catching up with the earlier drops and pushing them further down the pane. I should go up in the attic today. See what wonders that holds. Going through old stuff and memorabilia will soon take my mind off things. I've been putting it off in case of spiders which I'm sure must dwell up there. I have a great fear of them physically abusing me should I disturb them by jumping out and crawling on me or almost as bad the psychological abuse of them hanging in a corner looking menacing. Now, however, they seem the least of my worries.

I finish my tea and then brave the rain to find a ladder in the tiny shed in the corner of the garden and run with it into the house, heaving it carefully up the stairs and then propping it against the hatch in the ceiling.

The attic is small and cobwebby just as feared but actually there is a little more space than I expected and an electric light makes it easier to see all the treasures which await me. The naked bulb swings from one of the rafters as a draught catches it, casting light and shadow across the room. The rain is louder up here, hammering on the roof like rusty nails being shaken from a pot but I am pleased to see that, despite the rush of air I can feel from somewhere, there seem to be no drips coming through the roof. All is dry and dust.

The first thing I notice is the big wooden rocking horse. It is dapple with a thick black mane and tail and leather saddle. Its mouth is red and open displaying a block of viscous teeth gnashing at its bit. Its eyes are glassy and round and look as if, were I to jump on it, they would roll in its head wildly before it gallops off with me through some imaginary forest or desert plain. I wonder if I played on it as a kid. I'm sure I would have if I had been allowed. If only it could talk and tell me.

Yeah that would be good Elena I think. *Add a talking horse to your list of delusions.*

I stroke my fingers through its wiry mane before going further into the room. Old books are stacked in two piles from floor to ceiling, some gardening books; some obsolete encyclopaedias. I picture a door to door salesman being happy with his sale of them before Google made him and his kind redundant. There are novels too, faded and torn at the edges but good solid hardbacks all the same. I look along their spines at the names of the authors but recognise none. I take one from the top of the pile and wipe away the dust from its cover and reveal the kitsch, retro illustration depicting a couple from the 1800s in a passionate embrace, all bodices and buckles and heaving breasts. Definitely not my kind of book but it makes me smile. I imagine my aunt getting caught up in the romance and melodrama of it all. I never thought of her as having anyone special in her life. I have no idea if it was always that way. Maybe she preferred the stories to the reality. Maybe she died still hoping she'd meet someone who might change that.

I place the book back on the pile and look around to see what other clues about her life I can find. Some pictures lean against the wall. I flick through them though they are heavy in their frames and I wonder how many I can pull forward before the weight gets too much and I have to push them back before they fall on me. They are mostly landscapes, a couple of spaniels and one portrait of a lady in a blue Edwardian dress. Like the books I may come back to these or I may just leave them for whoever buys the house from me. They may even be pleased of the treasure trove. As I push them back though, I notice there is something familiar about the landscapes and they have a similar style to the painting in the lounge downstairs. I look at them more carefully. One is of the village with the church dominating the skyline and I see that one is almost certainly the beach at the end of the coastal path in the woods. Although in this picture the tide is out, not how I saw it, and there is a crowd of people looking out to sea at a tiny boat in the distance. I read the initials CR written at the bottom of both but it is only when I notice the easel propped in the corner that I realise my aunt must have painted these.

I go over to it. It is supporting a canvas which has been covered by a paint splattered sheet. I pull the sheet away, coughing as it billows dust into the air and I see the lake.

For a moment I forget to breathe.

It is just as ominous in the painting as it is in reality, perhaps more so as my aunt has painted a figure standing beside it, dressed all in black and veiled, her head bowed though there is something transparent about her. The black fades to grey as it sweeps away from her as if her clothes are smoke and her head is thin as if it too is draining away. I do not know if my aunt meant for it to look this way as it seems she did not finish the painting. A corner is still blank canvas, the brush strokes trailing into nothing.

I do not believe in ghosts or the paranormal, maybe when I was a child but certainly not now, however, obviously my aunt felt there was something wrong with that lake the same as I do otherwise why paint such a thing. And didn't Will say it had claimed a life before? I chalk it up to its gruesome past and an overactive imagination running in the family that has given us similar dark thoughts about the place. Nothing more sinister or strange, but still I place the sheet back across the canvas hiding it from view.

Then I come to the large trunk beside it. It is painted white and similar to the one in the spare room but bashed and chipped with the years. A huge lock hangs on the front but it is unfastened. I slip it from its latch and slowly open the lid which is heavy and creaks just like I hoped it would.

Inside are photo albums, big and bulky. I haul one out and open it. The cellophane protecting the pictures crackles pleasingly, reminding me of childhood visits to relatives who treasured all their photos like this and proudly presented them to friends and family after holidays and occasions. I remember holding the albums with reverence just as I am doing now and being reminded that I have to be careful not to touch the photos in case I get finger marks on them. I must be maybe nine in these memories and they are from after I left here though still I feel somehow distanced from them like they are not truly my own.

The people who stare back at me from the pictures are yellowed with age. They wear straight simple dresses and large brimmed hats. Some look serious and proud all posed for a family photograph. I recognise no one. I pull out another album, this one from more recent years. The photos are the faded hazy kind of the seventies, looking as though everything has been taken with an orange filter and grinning children with bowl haircuts look back at me. Again I have no clue as to who these people are. I flick through the pages and the photos become less faded and grainy. Now I see a picture of this house. It is resplendent with wisteria growing around the windows and doors. I recognise my mother standing by the door and feel a pang of loss looking at the happier, healthy version of the woman I said goodbye to two years ago. And there I am, maybe five years old. I have never seen a photo of me this young. My front teeth are missing making my lips curl and my eyes are full of laughter. I can't imagine the little girl I am looking at now causing any kind of problem for a village. She is full of life and I can't help but smile back at her, my fingers lightly touching the image, wishing I could go back and protect her from life, protect her from whatever happened to make her forget this very moment in the photograph when she was so full of joy and innocence. But protect her from what exactly I still have no idea.

    I feel better though somehow, looking at images of a forgotten time and seeing that they are normal, just a normal child with her mother. I'm not sure what I expected and hadn't even acknowledged the slight trepidation I'd had when opening these albums as to what I might find. I know that I am fearful of the past but this is a past which holds no demons I can see.

    Then I turn the page.

    In the next picture I look different. There are dark circles beneath my eyes and I stare at the camera, sullen and moody. I feel a chill run down my spine as I look into my own face, the eyes like an abyss pulling me down and I have to look away. I gasp for breath and realise my pulse is racing but have no idea why this image has brought on a panic attack. I turn the page quickly. Whatever memory was about to surface I am not ready for it yet. Not in this dark attic, not after seeing the horrible accident from earlier. Not when I am still recovering from everything else.

I close my eyes, taking deep breaths through my nose and blowing them out through pursed lips until my racing heart feels under control. But as I open my eyes and look at the next picture in the album it is as if my whole world has flipped and somersaulted as my mind tries to process what I am seeing.

Now there are two of me in the photo, two little girls side by side. Matching white frilly dresses, matching long dark hair falling just beyond their shoulders with the front sections clipped back, matching white socks and black patent shoes. All matching, all exactly the same, except one child is happy and one seems much more troubled and I cannot tell which one is me.

I had a sister. How could I have forgotten I had a sister?

Chapter 11

I do not know how long I spend in the attic. Hours? The way my life has just changed it may as well have been days, years. The albums pile up before me. Picture upon picture of two little girls, identical in features and yet always one seems troubled while the other is a normal happy child.

I even found names scribbled on the back of one of the photographs; Elena and Elsbeth.

Elsbeth. My sister's name was Elsbeth.

And in all I do not know which one I am. All I know is that I pray I am not the darker of the two. In many pictures I cannot even look at her. I can't explain the feeling I get when I look into her eyes but it is a primitive fear and a pounding starts in my head and a sickness washes over me and I have to turn the page before I can focus again, before I can breathe again.

I pray it is not my own eyes which I am looking into which are making me feel this way but I cannot be certain of this at all.

Why do I not remember a sister? What happened to me that I would forget?

More importantly what happened to her?

My mother has been dead two years and now my aunt has also passed away. There is no one left to ask who likely knows the whole story. I never knew my father. Our father, I correct myself and feel a shiver down my spine. There were never photos in the house of me before the age of seven. Why did I never think that strange? Why did I never question more?

Because something deep within me knew that I shouldn't. Whatever happened all those years ago meant I readily accepted my past being hidden. I never questioned too deeply, never wondered too much.

Now I've had enough of hiding. I need to know the truth and I don't want it sugar coated. If there are people who want me out of the village I want to know why. I want to know what they remember. Guessing at the truth is not an option anymore, nor is hiding from it. Not now I know how high the stakes are. Not now I know I lost a twin sister with whom I must have spent the first years of my life.

I realise that I have come to the end of the last album. I scrabble desperately in the trunk for more clues. There are a few photos trapped in the bottom but nothing that help me figure out what might have happened and nothing more is written on the back of any of them to explain which of the girls is me and which is my sister. I study the last photo, two little girls on the beach, matching red and white striped bikinis, a bucket and spade between them beside a half collapsed sandcastle. I make myself look at both children even though one fills me with dread but apart from the gut reaction to her image, to my image perhaps, nothing comes from staring at it. No sudden recollection, no flicker of recognition. Nothing.

I drop the picture to the floor in frustration and cast my hand about the chest once more. No more photos are left in the trunk now, they are all scattered around me, tormenting me, making me feel even more lost and empty and confused. Coming back here, going through old stuff, was supposed to help me to remember, to get back to happier times but all it has done is given me more questions. Questions I didn't even know needed asking. If I didn't feel grounded before due to my lack of early memories, now I feel as if I am hurtling through space with nothing to grab onto however hard I try. How? How could I have forgotten so much?

All that remains in the trunk now are newspaper clippings. I pick one out not expecting it to have any meaning for me. If the photos have not jogged any memory I doubt anything else will. I look at it anyway and see the date on it would have put me at about five years old. The headline is about a hunting tragedy. A gun backfired killing a local farmer, Philip Harvey, who had been out hunting rabbits.

Again my world tips.

I do remember this.

And I am in a field, running through the long grass which comes above my waist and feeling the sun on my face as I look up at the sky, squinting into its rays. In my mind the drifting pollen around me are fairies taking flight and I pretend that I am going to catch one and then persuade her to share her secrets of magic and mystical kingdoms with me. Then she will use her magic on me so that I become like her and we will be sisters and fly away across the fields and villages and into the woods where others like her dwell in castles within the trees and in cities made from flowers. The pollen orbs seem to shimmer as they float in the afternoon light, glowing golden against a pale blue sky and the grass tickles at my bare legs and arms as I run amongst them imagining that I am already flying. Somewhere I think I hear a car back fire and a dog barks in the distance but neither distracts me from the imaginary world I have created.

Then something does shatter my fantasy.

I stop running. There is a grey lump at my feet, limp with fresh blood on its side. A rabbit. Its eyes still bulge from terror even in death and its muzzle is wet with frothy spittle.

I gasp coming out from my childhood memory for a moment and thinking of the toy in the guest room last night, ragged and lifeless just like the rabbit I was staring at all those years ago.

I look at the paper again. At the grainy picture of the farmer gazing back at me, eyes too close together, cheeks ruddy and puffed out and I do not care that he died in such a way for I am five years old again trying to understand what has happened to the animal before me. And then I hear the gunshot reverberating through the air and I see the rabbits running, mothers and babies who had been as happy spending their time in the sunshine as I just moments ago. And then I see him, striding towards them, holding his gun high to take his aim and in that moment I hate him.

And another shot rings out and he is no more.

This memory is more real to me than any I have had since then. More visceral. Only my memory of Will and me as children compares to it in clarity and yet I cannot explain why. How can a forgotten past suddenly seem more mine than anything that happened after it, not only what happened on the roof in London which I wish was not real but also my job, my flat, friends, my entire adult life. None of it seems quite true compared to this one enduring image and it terrifies me in a way that I do not understand. A moment ago I was disconsolate that I couldn't remember anything. Now I am not sure that I want to.

Something is wrong with me and has been for a very long time.

I am not myself.

Chapter 12

I do not look at any more clippings, instead I slam the trunk shut. It can keep for another day for I have enough to think about and I feel that any more memories as intense as the one I just had may tip me over the edge. Instead I decide to meet Will down at *The Lady of the Lake*. He must have known my sister. He must have some answers even if it is unlikely he knows the full reason her existence was hidden from me. He will surely not be able to confirm, however, my fears that my mother may have purposefully erased my memories of whatever happened. Was I taken to some hypnotist? Forced to forget my sister? Forced to forget whatever I did so that I could live a normal life? Is that why coming back here has caused me to lose days, to think that I am losing my mind? Because I have remembered at some point and the shock has sent me into some kind of confusion where my whole mind shuts down until once again I am oblivious to what happened? Could that really be the reason and if so how bad does a memory have to be to cause that kind of thing? The thought terrifies me.

I feel my hands shaking as I go into the pub and suddenly I don't want to ask Will anything but then I see him sat at the bar, his deep blue eyes are warm and twinkle in the cosy light and a smile plays on his lips as he sees me and I cannot help but smile back. There is something about him which makes me feel safe.

'You want a drink?' he offers as I perch on a bar stool beside him.

'Yes, please. I definitely need one.'

His brow creases slightly and I can see his concern before he clearly decides not to question me further and orders me a double whisky and soda. I never told him what I wanted and yet he could not have judged it better. I see Sally grin as she squirts the soda into the glass, her eyes flicking to me and then to Will and back again. We'll be the next village gossip no doubt but that doesn't seem to be such a bad thing compared to what I imagine might otherwise be on people's tongues. She puts the drink in front of me with a wink and then hurries out into the kitchen.

'I'm glad you called. I was worried about you,' Will admits a little awkwardly, shifting on his barstool. 'Did you manage to get some sleep after I left?'

'Not really,' I sigh taking a sip of my drink.

'Me neither.' He looks down at the bar, the hand not on his pint flipping a tatty cardboard coaster between his fingers and I'm sure I can see his cheeks colouring a little.

'Sorry Will.'

He lets the coaster slip from his fingers, his attention now all on me. 'You have nothing to be sorry for Elena.'

'Not everyone appears to think that way.' I take another drink, grateful for the sweet warmth of the alcohol and knowing it may just numb me enough to keep it together until I can sleep and if I'm lucky maybe even keep away the dreams when I do.

'Have you had any more trouble from those men? Anybody else said something to you?' There is an edge to his voice, protective and I appreciate it.

'No. No more trouble.' I think about telling him about the toy on my floor but I don't want to get into what that may have been about right now, not when I have more pressing things I want to ask him.

'Good and you shouldn't be worrying about what they said either. They can't force you to leave.'

'I know that. I'm not worried about them. I've dealt with worse.'

'You have?'

I manage a smile, 'I work for a large firm in London Will. There are plenty of people around who would throw me off the ladder just to get to the next rung.'

He looks slightly puzzled but I guess being a self employed gardener down here doesn't mean he meets with the same kind of cut throat competition that I do.

'Then you just need to put yesterday behind you.' He takes a gulp of his beer like it is a punctuation mark. The discussion over, the matter closed.

'I'm trying to. I am.'

'But,' he prompts.

'But...' I go to take another sip of my drink, studying the liquid for a minute, swirling it around in the glass before deciding to just ask Will what I need to.

'Will, do you remember my sister?'

He is silent and looks at his pint as if that can give him an answer.

'Will, please tell me if you remember her.'

'Yes, yes I remember her,' he looks at me, then frowns, a realisation dawning in his eyes and I feel a little like an experiment he is trying to figure out. 'But I take it you don't.'

I shake my head, feeling the trembling in my hands return to my whole body. He studies my face a moment longer and I wait for him to say more but instead he goes back to looking at his pint, stroking his hands up and down the glass, wiping the condensation from it.

'Will, why don't I remember her? How can I have forgotten a twin sister? I found photos today. I mean, we were so alike I can't even tell which one is me and yet…' I take a breath feeling better now the words are out. The questions asked. He hesitates, his hand stilling on the glass and seems about to speak when there is a shout from the other end of the pub.

'She shouldn't even still be here!'

We turn around to see a burly man staring at us, maybe in his thirties, with round dark eyes and a tiny mouth hidden beneath a proboscis nose. He looks to be no stranger to fighting, all muscle but rolled in fat. One of his friends, a gawky individual with sandy hair who looks like someone has grabbed his head and pulled it up, stretching his neck so that it is all veins and sinews, has grabbed his arm and is rubbing his back, telling him to be quiet and trying to keep him in his seat. The other two men at the table look our way then comment to each other but I cannot work out what it is they are saying. One leans forward to also try and make the burly man stay in his seat and grey fish eyes sweep across me, calculating but it is the slight amusement in them which leaves me more disturbed.

'Well she shouldn't. Don't take a rocket scientist to work out it was her fault,' the man continues though more quietly now, begrudgingly heeding his friends as he clumsily shakes off their grips. His words are slurred and I notice his movements awkward as he settles back into his chair looking immediately for another swig of his pint.

I turn quickly back to my drink wanting to pretend they are not talking about me though I notice that Will does not. He just keeps staring at them and how can I pretend the comments were not aimed at me when the man was clearly looking at me and after the warnings I have received. But what exactly do they think is my fault? The missing girl again? How can they possibly think that I am responsible for that?'

'Don't mind them,' Sally comes quickly over to our end of the bar like a protective mother hen. She wipes the bar tap in front of us with a cloth and looks over at the men in disdain. 'Just stupid, superstitious men, always have been. You have your drink. Any more trouble and I'll make sure they leave.'

'Thank you,' I say, though the fact she also realises that they were talking about me makes me feel even more uncomfortable. I notice Will glance back at them again, his mouth is now a thin line and there is a viciousness in his expression which I haven't seen before, the warmth gone from his eyes, and I wonder how exactly he might have broken his nose in the past. Maybe not just from some sporting accident as I had presumed for the look on his face now makes me reconsider my thoughts yesterday that he would not have been a match for the men on my doorstep. I look back at Sally.

'What do you mean by they are superstitious? What has that got to do with me?'

'They just don't like newcomers tis all. Think bad things happen when outsiders come into the village, like bad things don't happen anyways.'

'You mean like the girl who went missing?'

'That,' she nods, 'And the council members.'

'Council members?' Will questions, his attention suddenly back on Sally rather than the men in the corner.

'Yes, haven't you heard? Three of them killed in a freak accident last night. Car was hit by a tree. On your road as it happens,' she gestures to me.

I feel as if all the air has been sucked out of the room and my mind whirs with the sudden realisation; the Land Rover, the same car that the men who threatened me last night drove off in. That was what I saw today.

An image of Geoffrey flashes into my mind, so proud he was helping the police in finding the girl, so sure of himself when he was ordering me to leave and return to London, and then the figure slumped in the car. I know he had been driving. I know it was him who I saw impaled. I take a gulp of my whisky, welcoming the burning sensation as it goes down.

'How can that be Elena's fault?' Will scoffs, looking back at the men again. 'They were in the wrong place at the wrong time, shouldn't have even been on that road on a night like it was last night. Don't even know what they were doing there.'

I do, I think, and so does Will.

'Well like I said, superstitious nonsense. If they had half a brain cell between them they'd be dangerous. Anything more out of them and I'll kick them out. I'll have a word with them now.'

Sally comes out from behind the bar and strolls over to the table the men are sat at still holding her cloth and I fully expect if given too much trouble she will spin it around and flick them with it. I watch her for a minute then turn back to Will not wanting to see their accusatory looks again if they notice me staring or hear their protests at whatever she is saying to them.

'Will did you see those council men when you left my place last night?'

He shakes his head, taking another sip of his drink.

'No, I walked back across the moors. I wanted to get home as quickly as possible with the weather like it was.'

I didn't know there was a way across the moors.

'Do you think it happened as soon as they left? Do you think they were sat on that road waiting for you to leave?'

'I don't know.' His voice is husky, distant.

I think of them parked beneath the tree, congratulating each other on getting into my house, on planting the toy there to scare me. Maybe one of them was about to announce his next idea to make me flee before the tree fell and silenced them all forever.

'Will this is more than me just being a newcomer isn't it?' I say quietly, not wanting the men in the corner to overhear. 'What happened to me back when I was little? What did I do that this village remembers and I don't?'

'Nothing Elena, you did nothing.'

'Then what happened to my sister? Will if you remember anything you have to tell me.'

Again he stares at his glass and it seems an eternity before he answers.

'She died,' he says simply, taking a deep drink of his pint and slamming the glass back onto the bar.

I knew this, of course I knew it. Where else could she be and yet it hits me harder than I can believe. I never knew I had a sister until a few hours ago and now I feel the loss almost as if I had known her all my life.

'How?' I manage.

'She drowned.' Again the words are just said as if Will is telling me she simply moved away or they just lost touch but I can see the glassiness in his eyes and know he is holding back tears.

'What happened? I mean, when, where?'

'I don't know the details Elena; just that she drowned. Can we just leave it at that?'

No, I think, we can't and I don't know that I want the answer to the next question but it comes out anyway.

'Was it my fault?'

'No,' Will looks at me, his mouth that thin line again and anger flashing in his eyes though I have no idea why or whether it is aimed at me. 'No it wasn't your fault. None of it was ever your fault.'

'None of what?'

'I can't deal with this right now Elena. OK.' He downs the dregs of his pint and shrugs on his jacket.

'Deal with what Will?' Now it is my turn to be angry. This is my life I'm trying desperately to figure out, my lost childhood. If he knows something what right does he have to keep it from me?

'Any of it.'

'And you think I can? I've just found out that my entire past has been a lie. Don't you think I have a right to know why?' I grab his arm as he tries to walk past me and make him face me. I see one previously held back tear fall down his cheek as he studies my face as if searching for something though I am unsure what. Maybe for her, my sister, I think and an inexplicable jealousy rushes through me.

'You're back now,' he says quietly. 'Can't that just be enough?'

'No,' I shake my head, softening in the wake of his obvious grief. 'No it can't.'

'Then I can't help you.' He shakes off my grip and walks out the door. I stare at it as it slams closed, convinced if I keep watching it I will somehow make him return but I finish my drink alone and then leave myself, only briefly glancing at the now empty chairs where the abusive man and his friends had been sat. I hadn't even noticed them leave.

Chapter 13

As I walk home the moon intermittently gets obscured by clouds, plunging me into darkness and shadow before reappearing and bathing the path in silver once more. I wrap my jacket around me a little tighter and stride forward, not really paying attention to my route home, so lost am I in my own thoughts. That is until I am almost at the place where I saw the Land Rover earlier today. Then I do pay attention although I don't want to, so I keep my head down and try hard not to notice the remnants of the ripped trunk where the tree which killed those councillors snapped from. The shards of wood and bark rising up from it like spikes and reminding me of exactly how the men died. I walk quickly past, doing my best to block the image of their deaths from my mind and yet still dark thoughts slip into my head. Did all of them die instantly or did they linger? Did one fight for life longer than the others, trapped by the branch as he bled out, unable to move or cry for help? Only able to stare at his dead companions and know he would be joining them very soon. I swallow and shake my head as if that will help shake off the images. Whatever happened they are at peace now. Their last moments and last thoughts will never truly be known and maybe that is a good thing. Maybe we shouldn't know.

The path bends and I'm pleased now that even if I look back I will not be able to see the place where it happened. Instead my thoughts turn to my sister again and how I could have forgotten her. I wonder how much Will really knows and why he is so reluctant to tell me anything and I wonder why a village hates me. And the clouds sweep across the moon once more and the night darkens again and that is when I see her.

She stands on the path in front of me, long hair dancing in the wind, shining blonde strands covering her face. She looks to be about five and I know then that it is the missing girl although even in shadow I can see something about her face seems older than it should, as if she has seen far more than her five years would ever have allowed.

I take a step towards her, not wanting to frighten her though I wonder who is more scared right now, her or me.

'Hey honey, what are you doing out here? Don't you think we should get you home?' I call out but she still does not acknowledge me, her eyes are fixed on the ground. Of course she is the one who is more scared. Who knows what has happened to the poor kid or why she hasn't been found until now. I take another step towards her and notice the dirty toy bunny clutched in her hand; the one that was in my cottage. One eye still hangs loose spinning on its single thread and a drop of water falls from one of its feet and splashes on the ground. I stop walking and stare at it, at her pale hands clutching it, her nails torn and filthy. And the wind whips her hair back from her face as the moonlight illuminates the path once more and finally she looks up at me, glaring; her eyes blacker and larger than they should be.

'Don't let her take me,' she rasps and the voice is that of a child but there is something else there, like a second voice behind it. Not an echo exactly, in fact hardly a voice at all, more of a creaking. And an image flashes into my mind of rusted old graveyard gates swinging back and forth in a growing storm allowing the living to enter and the dead to escape. It whispers the lines to the girl a split second before she says them. 'Give her back what is hers.'

I open my mouth to reply but no words come and then I hear the shout behind me. It breaks the spell the child has on me and I turn to see the drunk from the pub earlier. He is staggering towards me, a thick branch in his hand. Perhaps he found it lying on the road from where they cleared the accident. I don't know but I am instantly reminded of being on the roof and Nathan coming towards me with the hammer. The same enraged look in his eyes, the same way he holds the would-be weapon. Feeling the weight of it, imagining the possible destruction and pain it could cause. And I have the same certainty that there is no reasoning to be had, that this man also means to hurt me or worse.

I turn to run and to tell the girl to do the same but she is no longer standing in my path, she has vanished once more along with the moonlight and I have no idea where she went and no time to worry about it. It is only a little further to my cottage and the man is drunk, I should have little trouble outrunning him. I can get inside and call the police and just pray they come in time before he smashes my windows with that branch.

My feet smack on the hard ground, echoing into the night and it is all I can hear until his footsteps join them, growing louder behind me. Now they are all I can focus on. Is he catching up to me? I dare not look; even a glance and I could stumble in this darkness. I see my gate up ahead. Only a little further. A little further and I should be safe. I feel for the keys in my pocket and wrap my hand around them reassuringly as my house comes into view, looming up like a safe haven behind the trees.

And as the moon once more shines out from behind the clouds I see the others, the other men from the pub. All three of them by my gate. Waiting for me.

The panic I feel spears through me and makes me almost falter but there is no time for hesitation and, praying that they have not seen me, I change direction, heading into the woods but I hear a shout and know that they are after me and they are not as drunk as their friend. They will easily catch up with me and then what? Are they just going to ask me politely to leave like the men did from last night? I somehow doubt it. And then as if to confirm my fears I hear what they are shouting to each other.

'I am going to have fun with this.'

'Can you even remember how to have fun with a woman?'

'You shut up, I'll remember fine, let's just catch the bitch. '

'Shouldn't be too hard out here. She's that thin she looks like she will snap.'

There is laughter.

'I can't wait to test that theory.'

I feel sick. This can't be happening to me. I can't let it.

I run faster terrified of tripping but it is as if the woods are clearing for me, the tree branches lifting, the track smoothing out with none of the usual roots and twigs as obstacles. They will soon catch me though. I can hear twigs snapping behind me and then worse than the shouts or the footsteps I can now hear their breaths, ragged and husky as their lust and hate drives them on. Tears start to prick my eyes as the horror of what is about to happen if they catch me seeps in. My only option is to get off the path and so I dart into the trees, clutching at the trunks to steady me as I weave in and out, trying to focus and ignore the despair that I will never get away.

Now all I can hear is my own breathing and after a few minutes I slow a little, listening out for a crunch of leaves or a thud of footsteps but there is nothing. I don't think they saw me come off the path. Hopefully they have run straight past down to the lake or to the beach and I can make my way back to the house and call the police. I listen for a bit longer, leaning up against the trunk of a huge oak tree and gasping air back into my burning lungs, straining to hear anything but all is silent apart from the buzzing in my ears caused by the anxiety I am feeling. I dare not head back to the path. Not quite yet.

    I reach in my pocket suddenly remembering my mobile. I can call from here and wait for the police to come before attempting to head back where the men might see me. I cradle the phone almost dropping it my hands are shaking so much. It is too dark to recognise me and it buzzes obstinately as it takes me three attempts to tap in my password, having to clear my mind and focus the best I can on the last attempt so that I don't risk locking the phone. Finally the home screen slides into place showing me all the helpful apps that I can use and telling me that there is no signal at all. I dial 999 anyway but nothing happens. No network is all I am told. I dial again, pressing the phone to my ear.

    'Comeoncomeoncomeon,' I mutter, 'please ring, please answer. Please.' But the line is dead, there is nothing. I wait a few more moments willing it to suddenly connect but all is silence. It is hopeless. I scan the woods, looking through the trees at the direction I came. Everything is still. I have to get back to the house if I am to call for help but the thought of heading back is terrifying. I can't. Not yet. And so, without thinking, I wander from the tree holding the phone out in front of me, hoping to capture just the faintest whisper of service which will be enough for an emergency call at least and it glows out in the darkness like a beacon and I hear the shouts resume.

'There, she's over there!'

And once more I am running. I clasp the phone in my hand. How could I have been so stupid as to let them see it but maybe I can use it as a bluff? Tell them the police are on their way but I have no doubt that living here for years they will know there is no way I could have called for help. Not in these woods. I am heading deeper and deeper into the trees and don't even know which direction I am pointing now. Is the ground suddenly going to give way? Am I going to plummet over the cliff at any moment in the darkness, to lose them only to have the sea claim me? I cannot hear the ocean though, all I can hear is them rustling through the branches and they are gaining on me. The shouts have stopped as they no doubt save their breath for the chase. There is determination in their silence. This is a hunt and they do not mean to lose their quarry.

I glance back and cannot see them and I hope that means they can also not see me. I change direction once more, veering off to the right. The grass is much higher here, the ground more uneven. It slows me down but seems a better bet than trying to outrun them on the flatter terrain. This time I do trip though, falling to my knees. I hoist myself up and half run, half crawl across the undulating ground. The dampness from the grass seeps through my clothes chilling me and I manage to put my phone back in my pocket to keep it from getting wet, still hoping that perhaps I will get the chance to use it again and be able to call for help.

As I scramble over a fallen log I hear the whisper of grass behind me and am sure they have managed to follow me. I start to doubt that I am ever going to escape this.

They are never going to give up. But neither am I. I push myself forward doing my best to run through the thick foliage. The ground suddenly drops in front of me and I slide down it, leaves and mud flying up at me and I don't know how I manage to stifle a scream as I tumble, trying to slow myself by keeping my legs out in front of me, unable to see what lies at the bottom of the slope in the darkness. I grab at roots and grass but all slip through my hands leaving nothing but moss and slime on my palms. I land on my back and take a moment to catch my breath, looking around to see where I am. Mud banks surround me. Am I in the lake? Have they drained it to try and find the girl?

'No. Nonononono,' I whimper, fear of a different kind piercing through me as I shuffle backwards, waiting for something to claw its way out from the dirt. To have been expecting me. I turn to where I just fell and try to crawl back up, my hands grasping at the wet mud and grass but then common sense prevails and I let myself slide back down. This is not the lake and even if it were I am safer down here than out there. If I can just stay hidden the men may not notice. They may go straight past the hollow or not see me in the darkness and think that I would have scrambled my way out of it if I had come this way. I try to press myself into the side of the bank but I can hear them coming and I see a torch beam lancing across the sky above me.

'Where'd she go?'

'Come out come out wherever you are.' I hear one of them laugh.

'We tain't going to hurt you, not much,' another calls out. 'You might even enjoy yourself being as you're so keen to stay here an' all. Thought we could show you what the place has to offer.'

There is a shriek of laughter and I imagine them as hyenas, stalking back and forth above me, eyes gleaming in the moonlight, hungry for their prey, hunched and greedy and soulless.

I close my eyes as if blocking out the night will somehow also block me out of their sight. I dare not move. They are right above me. They are going to come across the incline at any minute and then they will find me and they will be upon me and I will have no way of escaping. And I have run so far into the woods that no one will hear my screams. No one will come and help me out here. They will win. I will return to London just as they want. I will bargain with them right now as long as they don't touch me. Anything to keep them from touching me. But I doubt there is any bargaining to be had with these men.

'Are you crazy? I wouldn't want to go near her like that. Who knows what diseases she might have picked up in the city.' I hear the drunken man who I had first seen on the path. He has caught up then. Now they are all here. All four.

'Fine you can just hold her for me then.'

'Yeah and me,' I hear another one laugh. 'You're too drunk to be able to manage anything much anyway.'

'You two just shut up. We need to find her first.'

I slow my breathing, trying to catch my breath and yet hardly daring to breathe in case they hear me. My eyes are still tightly shut though that does not keep the tears back which now run down my face. Any minute and they will see me. Any minute and that torch is going to shine down on me and I will be lost. I can't look. I can't. I move my lips in silent prayers. My fingers claw the earth digging into it and sinking into the soft mud as I press myself against the ground hoping to disappear into it as well.

And I feel something move.

It is not something physical but more like a shift in the atmosphere, like everything around me has become more alive and I hear the foxes scream and I hear the owls screech but the shouts of the men stop and there is silence.

And I feel sure that in it they will hear my ragged breaths and my heart which is thundering so loudly. That the silence has come from the fact they are looking right at me now as they make their way down the slope, trying not to laugh as I sit huddled not realising just how close they are and yet still I cannot look. Still I want to pretend that they will not find me, that I will somehow get away.

Then something hits my shoulder, hard, making my eyes fly open and I almost scream as I see it is the torch that one of them was holding. And it bathes me in blinding light before it comes apart as it clatters to the ground, the batteries coming loose and all is dark again. I stare at it expecting one of the men to jump down after it at any minute. That they must have seen me revealed in its light even if it was only for a second. And then their shouts come back even louder as if to confirm this but I realise this time they are not angry or lascivious. This time they are not for me. But they are screams more terrible than that of any fox, more horrifying to me somehow than any of their words before and I cannot bear to listen to their cries. I clap my hands over my ears so tightly I feel them burn and screw my eyes shut once more and realise I am rocking back and forth, back and forth, willing it to stop. Willing them to end.

And then silence.

I open my eyes. I feel drained but calm. The men are gone. Where I do not know but they are gone, of that I am certain. Then I do hear a voice.

'Elena?'

'Will?' I dare to look up from my hiding place and I see him looking down at me, his expression confused, terrified and I don't know how he is suddenly there but he is and that is all that matters right now. I crawl back up the slope, my feet sliding out beneath me on the loose earth and leaves. He reaches out his hand and I clasp it as he hauls me up beside him.

'I should never have left you,' he says and hugs me to him. I am still bewildered but wrap my arms around him and then the sobs come and we are both crying and I know my tears are from relief and maybe his are too but there is so much more to his sadness than I know. And as I cling to the safety of him I think he whispers something in my ear but I cannot be sure I heard it right.

'I should never have done this to you.'

might have been there. 'They won't believe you Elena, I'm sorry but they won't.'

'Just like they didn't believe that I saw that child in the lake.' I shrug him off irritated.

'I believe you Elena, don't think I'm saying that I don't.'

'Maybe you shouldn't.' I look down at my tea again, easier to admit that I may have been wrong to the cup in my hands than to Will who doesn't have to tell me that he believes me, I can see he does just from the way he looks at me. 'I know I didn't see the body of the missing girl now.'

'What do you mean?'

'Because I saw her tonight,' I say, glancing up at him again. 'Alive.'

'Are you sure?'

'I'm not sure of anything anymore but I saw a little girl on the path before the men tried to attack me. She was holding the same toy they said the girl had when she disappeared. I don't know where she went. They must have frightened her but someone should go out looking for her. I can't. I daren't. But someone should.'

Will says nothing.

'I think we should tell someone is all,' I continue, 'Maybe you're right though. They're certainly not going to believe me. I don't want to go through all that questioning again. I can't.'

'I know,' he agrees, placing his hand back on my arm, his touch reassuring, making me feel not so alone in everything I'm going through despite him only knowing a fraction of it.

'I think she's disorientated though. She was saying things that made no sense.'

'Like what?'

I think of the demand she gave me, to give something back. The way it had sounded, the threat behind the words and for some reason I can't bring myself to repeat them.

'It doesn't matter. Maybe those men saw her too. Maybe they helped her. It was me they wanted to hurt, not her. She wouldn't have been in any danger from them I don't think. Maybe finding her made their reasons for chasing me down less important. Or maybe she's what scared them. Sally said they were superstitious. Maybe they thought she was something more sinister than just a little girl at first.'

I certainly did.

Will doesn't answer me. Instead he gets up and takes his cup to the kitchen.

'Will,' I call suddenly nervous that he is about to leave, to go out to see if he can find the girl himself. 'Please stay a bit longer.'

I don't care if it sounds desperate or that I might inconvenience him. The thought of being on my own is too terrible right now. I should be more worried about the girl, I know I should, but there was something about her that makes me wonder if she was even real. Was she a part of those men's plan even? Just another thing to try and terrify me into leaving? It seems convenient that I saw her at that time and that even what she said sounded like a threat.

Will walks back into the room. I look up at him. 'I'm sure those men are going to come back,' I say. 'I don't understand what scared them so much but once whatever has distracted them is done with, they'll be back for me. I have no doubt.'

'They won't be coming back Elena.'

'How can you be so certain? You didn't see their faces Will. You didn't hear what they were saying.'

He sits beside me on the couch once more and takes hold of my face between his hands so that I am forced to look into his eyes, his pupils huge and dark in the warm glow of the room.

'They won't be coming back.'

I don't know how he can be so certain and I don't know what it means that he is and right now I don't want to care about either. I just want to forget what happened to me out in the woods, forget what's been happening to me since December and stop trying to control my emotions, pretending that I'm OK, pretending that I'm coping better. Pretending that I don't want or have these feelings for someone I feel I only met days ago and yet he has known me from childhood and maybe knows me better than I know myself.

And so as he draws my face to his I do not resist and when his mouth gently brushes against mine I want to sink into him, to get lost in him but then he pulls back.

'I'm sorry,' he says, blinking and shaking his head as if coming out of trance and suddenly realising his actions. 'I shouldn't have...' He turns away as if ashamed but I grab his hand before he can get up from the couch.

'Don't be.'

He turns back to me, his eyes smouldering in the fire light, questioning again, uncertain, but this time I know what he is asking and I know my answer. 'Don't be,' I whisper again as I move towards him, my heart racing as if I have never been in this situation before and I notice he seems to have the same trepidation as he hesitates before leaning into me, his eyes still searching my own, wanting to see that I am sure, that this is real. I reach up, cupping his cheek, and for a moment we just stay there, so close, hardly breathing, before his mouth sweeps across my own again, his lips tracing mine and it feels as if I have been waiting for this moment for eternity and every nerve inside my body comes alive and I cannot pull him close enough. At first his kiss is soft, tentative, but then as I respond so does he, and I feel his tongue reach into my mouth and his rough stubble against my face and my fingers clutch and entwine in his soft black hair as he devours me with the same urgency I am feeling. He pushes me back onto the couch so that I am trapped beneath him, kissing my face, my neck, my shoulders, pushing up my vest top and flicking his tongue down my stomach, his teeth grazing my skin, tugging at my flesh, sending volts through me and I bite my lip as each breath comes out a whimper. And as he stops to remove his t-shirt, I can't wait for him any longer and I sit up, finding his lips again with my own and pulling him down on top of me once more.

And as we come together I remember. I remember seeing him for the first time, two years older than me, on the beach running out of the surf. I had run towards him, wanting to talk with him, to be his friend, fascinated by him. And at first he was reluctant to play with me but then I must have said something to amuse him because I remember his smile and the way he looked at me, eyes twinkling with fun and a kind of curiosity and in no time at all we were laughing like children do at simple pleasures. Finding shells on the beach, him making me giggle so much when he pretended one was an eye patch as we explored caves and imagined we'd found pirate treasure. I remember going to his house for tea, eating slices of hot buttered saffron bread in winter and drinking ice cold glasses of chocolate milk with scoops of vanilla ice cream where are her teeth? Why is all I can see emptiness? And a voice rasps out of the chasm that is her throat, hissing, and the words are drawn out like when you try and scream in a dream but the effort it takes distorts everything.

'Geeeeeet ouuuuuuut.' And she shoves me so hard I fall backwards but before I hit the ground I wake.

'Getoutgetoutgetoutgetout!' the girl standing at the bottom of my bed screams at me. It is her, it is me; it is the missing girl. It is something much worse than anything I have known before and so I scream.

'Elena! Elena!' Will grabs me pulling me back to reality. 'Elena it's OK, you're safe.'

My breathing slows but I realise I am crying. I am still sat upright in the bed staring at where I just saw her.

'Am I?' I look at him, desperate for him to say the right thing but he does not. Instead he just hugs me and I feel the weight of the word he did not say. Yes was all I needed to hear but he didn't say it because I know, deep down I know, that he doesn't believe it. And neither do I.

Chapter 16

I am running through the woods. My heart is racing as my feet rush across the grass and weeds and I leap over the roots of the trees and I feel the cooling wind against my face in the hot sun. Is he catching up with me? Did he see where I went? I dare to glance behind but see no one. I know he is much faster than me but I took a sneaky way through the trees and past the ant hill which he once told me was like New York City for ants and where all the other ants aim to get to, to make it big. It means I've cut out the big corner where the path gets all curvy which should put me way ahead of him. He's going to know that I cheated but I'll tell him that I didn't and see if I can get away with it.

'Lena, I know you took a short cut!' I hear him call and I duck behind a tree, peering out to see if I can see him jogging along the path but all is still and I can't work out in which direction the shout came from. I wait for him to call again but the woods are quiet now. The only sound is the rustle of the leaves as the wind jostles them, sounding like waves washing up on the shore and as if I am nearer to the ocean than I am. I try and slow my breathing and stay silent too so I can work out where he is and he won't find me first. But he is always really good at finding me. My heart is pounding as I try to stay still and my tummy feels all squirlly waiting for him to appear. It always feels that way on the days I get to spend with my best friend though. He's taking ages to catch up. Surely I didn't get that far ahead of him and he didn't sound so far away when he shouted.

As I lean a little further out from the tree I see a squirrel. It chases down the trunk of a huge pine opposite and scuttles across the ground before sitting up and sniffing the air. I hope that it will come a little closer and it does turn to face me. I stay very still and it takes a few jerky steps towards me but then something spooks it and it flees the other way, a wave of fur disappearing up another tree and into the branches. And as I wonder what it saw that scared it so, I feel hands grab at my sides. I scream.

'Caught you!'

I turn to see Will and my already thumping heart now goes skippity hopping all over the place. He is one big grin and I am a little jealous of his smile as my front tooth is missing and although the tooth fairy did pay me for it I don't think she is being quick enough to make me a new one. Will is older than me though; a whole two years so the fairies replaced his teeth ages ago. Despite him being older he never makes me feel like a little kid. I feel proper grown up when I'm with him.

'You cheated!' he accuses me.

'I did not. It wasn't in the rules that we had to stay on the path.'

He considers this for a minute then digs his fingers into my ribs tickling me and I shriek and try and push him away though I don't try very hard.

'Don't think you can get the better of me, Lena. You know it won't work,' he laughs, still poking at me as I wriggle out of his grasp. 'It was still cheating.'

'I still got here first,' I say all breathless from the running and the attack on my ribs.

'You don't play fair,' he shakes his head and wanders through the trees and out into the clearing we were racing to. I go to follow him but then stop. I have not been this far

into the woods before and suddenly the safety of my aunt's cottage seems very far away.

A lake stretches out before us. It shimmers, bluey-green in the sunlight and it reminds me of the peacock feathers my Aunt Carol showed me once and how they changed colour when she turned them this way and that. But this is not beautiful like the feathers were and there is something about the water that makes me uncomfortable so I stay amongst the trees. For some reason I don't want to go any further and I watch Will uneasily as he crouches on the bank and starts to pick up sticks which he thinks will be good to build the model raft he'd talked about. He looks up at me when he realises that I'm not helping.

'Lena, what you doing? Why are you just standing there? Come and help me gather boat materials.'

'I'm happy here,' I shrug, hoping he'll think I've just changed my mind and won't think I'm being a chicken.

'What? Are you scared of something?'

'No!' How does he always know what I am feeling?

'Then get over here.'

'No, I'm good here.'

'What's wrong with you? You can swim can't you? You're not worried about falling in?' He gets up and comes towards me leaving his little pile of sticks on the ground.

'Yes of course I can swim. You've seen me swim Will.' I roll my eyes at him.

'Then why are you scared of a little lake.'

'I told you I'm not scared. I just don't like it here much. It feels weird.' I hug myself and feel the goosebumps on my arms despite the warm summer air.

'There's nothing wrong with this place.' He glances at the lake and then turns back to me. And I know he's trying to think of a way to persuade me to come closer when his

eyebrows furrow a little bit and then a crooked smirk appears on his face before he says, 'It's where I got my pet jellyfish.'

I narrow my eyes at him the way my mum sometimes does with me when she thinks I'm making stuff up. 'You don't have a pet jellyfish.'

'I do, and his name is Albert.'

'You don't have any pet called Albert and even if you did, jellyfish don't live in lakes. We did a project on fish at school. You find them in the ocean. '

'What about freshwater jellyfish?'

I frown, starting to doubt myself but I am not about to let Will get the better of me.

'Whatever. No jellyfish live in this lake.'

'Well no, not now, because they live at my house.'

'Not ever Will!' I can't help but smile as I shout at him.

'Albert did,' Will insists. Now his eyebrows go all up making his eyes even wider and rounder as if that will make it seem more like he's telling the truth and he's getting excited as he thinks up more things to try and get me to believe. 'This is where he was when I found him.'

'No you didn't.' I feel my lips trying to smile again so I put them together tightly as I know he's teasing me and wanting me to believe him and just waiting to tease me even more if I show any signs that I do or that I'm enjoying this conversation. I love it when he makes up stories though. Sometimes they are really stupid and not as good as my made up stuff about fairies and princesses but I don't really mention them when I'm with him in case I sound too childish.

'Yeah I did!' his voice gets high and squeaky as he pretends to be annoyed that I don't believe him.

His dad does the same thing. Not so much the squeakiness but he tells us loads of stories about heroic animals and talking trees and broccoli having feelings and being very sad if you don't eat it. And when we challenge him about it he acts as if he's upset that we think he's telling fibs. And I think he's really silly but I wish he was my daddy. Maybe when my real daddy comes and finds me he'll be good at telling stories too.

'He was scared of the ocean so his parents moved here when he was a baby so he would be happier,' Will continues.

'He wasn't scared of the ocean!' I want to tease him back and pretend I don't find him funny but I can feel little bubbles of laughter jumping around inside me and they are on their way up and I don't think I can stop them no matter how hard my lips are pressed together.

'He was! I promise you Lena. You don't know him like I do. You've never been round to tea at his house.' Will continues stepping away from me.

'Neither have you! And jellyfish don't even drink tea!' I go after him not wanting to end the discussion till I've got the better of him. 'They don't have mouths.'

'They do Lena, and we had scones with jam and cream.' He studies me, his eyes flashing with amusement, waiting for my reaction and to add to his make belief world.

'How did they get here then?' My words come out all jolty as I try desperately hard to sound sensible and catch him out without laughing. 'How did they make it here from the ocean?

'Duh, Lena, they've got a car.'

Now I do start giggling and I see Will smiling at me, and I know he's all pleased because he's acting like his dad and making me laugh.

'Jellyfish can't drive cars,' I manage through the giggles, shaking my head.

'No, that's true. They found that out after they got it but it was OK as they got Edward the cod fish to drive them.'

Still laughing I push him away from me. 'You're a cod fish,' I say.

'No you're a cod fish,' he pushes me back gently but then looks behind him. 'But not a scared cod fish anymore. Look, you're right up at the banks of the lake and nothing has happened to you.'

I look around and realise he is right. During his little story I forgot my fear and came out from the safety of the trees, so caught up listening to him I didn't realise that he was luring me out. The lake still frightens me for some reason but it doesn't seem so bad when Will is right beside me.

'See nothing to be scared of.' He picks up a stone and skims it across the surface. It bounces three times before hitting a lily pad and disappearing into the waters. He tried to teach me to do that once but mine just plop and sink.

'I wasn't scared,' I insist knowing that he doesn't believe me.

'Well even if you were, you don't have to be with me around.' He stands upright, shoulders back and head up so I can see how much he has grown recently and I know he is pleased with himself because he is the third tallest in his class now and he's hoping to reach six foot soon as that's how tall you have to be to be a fireman. 'I'll look after you Lena.' He skims another stone and then puts his arm

around me as he watches the little trail of splashes it makes. 'I'll never let anything bad happen to you. I promise.'

***

I wake but keep my eyes closed, clinging to how happy I have just been and how safe I have just felt in my dream before it dissipates as reality and consciousness take over, my childhood slipping away from me once more. I can't remember how long it has been since I wanted to stay in my dreams rather than escape them and I enjoy how relaxed I feel for once because of it. Last night it felt like I would never feel like this or stop being afraid and plagued by nightmares and I didn't think I would ever shake my feelings of despair even as Will held me in the darkness, stroking my hair until finally I fell back to sleep.

Will.

I remember this unusual feeling of happiness isn't just in my subconscious. We are together again, finally, and I open my eyes and reach out for him but his side of the bed is empty. I sit up panicking a little, hoping last night wasn't just a onetime deal; that he hasn't instantly regretted it. But then I see the note on his pillow. It says that he has a job to do, that he didn't want to wake me and that he will come back this evening if I want him to. I turn the note over and see that there is a sketch of a girl on the back, her eyes closed, her lips slightly parted and then I realise she is supposed to be me. I run my fingers across it and wonder how long he was awake, watching me sleep to draw this. In only a few pencil strokes he's made me look so peaceful with my hair cascading around me, so content. Maybe that was why I didn't recognise myself at first. It is not an expression I am used to seeing in the mirror. I smile as I touch my own features as he sees them and the way it is drawn reminds me somehow of the elfish faces in the painting downstairs.

I realise that I am no longer afraid that those men will come and find me. All seems better in the daylight and shafts of sun stream through the gaps in the curtains bathing everything in light and warmth. I'm also sure if it was the missing girl I saw last night she will have found her way home by now. All she needed to do was get to the end of the lane and she'd be in the village. I'll try and find out if there has been any news about her today and hopefully I won't have to worry about talking to anyone about what I saw.

I pull a gown around me and go over to the window, drawing the curtains back and look out at the garden below and another memory of Will and me as children hits me. They are coming thick and fast now like he opened the floodgates within me, unlocking my past though my sister still remains in the darkness. I think she may be on the periphery of my memories but I cannot be sure, like a presence rather than that she was physically there and again I wonder if I am forcing her into events in desperation to place her in my life rather than actually remembering her existence at all.

Now I see myself crouching next to the hedgerow. A vole rests in my hand, its breathing erratic and I can feel the tiny heart beating fast but then begin to slow. There is blood on its flank and half its tail has gone; a cat's game that has been discarded and left to die no doubt. I cup it in both hands and want to cry. Its tiny nose twitches and its eyes are closed, while its mouth is open, gasping in air as best it can. It is so small and so helpless and there is nothing I can do but I do not want it to die.

'What are you doing Lena?' Will comes over to me. 'Put that down, it's diseased.'

'It's not diseased, it's just wounded,' I state.

'Wounded, diseased, whatever. It's dirty and gross.'

'It's hurt and it's suffering,' I say and my voice trembles. Will sits beside me on the grass, his hair flopping over his eyes just like it does now.

'There's nothing you can do about it Lena. It's just life. These things happen.'

I ignore him and close my eyes and feel the little heartbeat in my hand getting fainter and fainter and I surround it with warmth and I think about how much I want to bring life back to it. I can hardly feel the heart now, just a few more erratic beats and then I am sure it has stopped but I am not ready to give up so I continue to imagine that it hasn't, that it is still pumping, flooding life around the little body in my hands. And the outside world floats away and then all I can see is pulsating red in the darkness, small at first and then growing larger, until I feel a movement against my finger tips. At first just a flutter so I am unsure whether I have imagined it but then it comes again. A heartbeat, growing stronger and stronger until it is consistent once more and then I feel tiny claws against my palm, scratching to get out. I open my eyes, carefully parting my hands and putting them down on the ground quickly as the vole scuttles from them and disappears into the long grass.

'How did you…?' Will gasps. I just smile.

I smile now remembering how powerful I felt after that and believing that maybe, just maybe I had a little fairy magic in me. Of course now I know that the vole probably wasn't as hurt as I had thought and was likely just in shock and needed a moment before it was fine to escape again, no mystical forces at work at all. I wonder if Will remembers that time though. I shall ask him this evening.

I walk out of the bedroom passing the spare room. I should remove that toy for I know it cannot be the same one the girl was holding last night but a replica used as a warning and therefore must still be where I left it. I will show it to Will and see if he agrees with me that it was placed there to try and frighten me, for what other reason could there be? Not that it really matters now I suppose, not now that the men who I am sure put it there are no more. Though if that is the case and the reason they were under that tree when it fell, their punishment certainly did not match their crime.

I open the door and look at the centre of the floor where the toy should have been lying but it has gone with not so much as a mark on the carpet where it had rested, soaking and stinking. I walk into the room scanning for it. Maybe Will came in here earlier and picked it up though I cannot see where he would have put it. I will ask him later for I am not going to consider the alternative, that it was the same one clutched in the child's hands last night. That somehow she or someone else managed to get back into my house to retrieve it. Right now I am just glad it is gone. I didn't want to touch it again. At least now I don't have to worry.

As I pass the shelf beside the bed I see a silver box nestled between several teddy bears and the porcelain dolls. There is a familiarity about it which I did not notice before. I pick it up, running my fingers across the cool embossed images of children playing on its outer casing. I feel as if my hands know each crevice of this box already like I have handled it many times, feeling the smooth curves of the boys' faces, the ribbons sweeping from the girls' hair. I open it to find that it is lined with red velvet, two figures dancing at its centre, black silhouettes against a crimson sky. And a chime rings out as the lid folds back.

I shudder remembering the chimes in the woods but quickly decide that I'd be pretty disappointed in myself if I let that memory make me afraid of a music box. I also resist the urge to turn the porcelain dolls away from me so that I don't have to look into their vacant eyes. Somehow the thought of them with their backs to me, staring at the wall, is even more unsettling than them watching me. I wonder if I was fond of them as a child. I vaguely remember being so in a dream I had but I am not sure that means I truly was and they certainly hold no sentimentality for me as the box in my hand now does.

Closing the lid I turn it upside down and find a winding mechanism. It produces a satisfying clicking noise as I turn it as far as it will go and then carefully put the box down and open the lid once more to hear what tune will play.

Girls and Boys come out to play rings out in the room and the tune is comforting, nothing like what I heard in the woods. It is childhood and innocence and safety.

I smile placing it carefully back on the shelf, watching the figures twirl for a few more moments before leaving it to play out. I go back out onto the landing, shutting the door behind me and briefly catching my reflection in the mirror on the opposite wall. There is something strange about it. My face looks contorted as if it has been pencil drawn and then someone has smudged it, wiping their hand across the image as if an attempt to destroy what they have just created. I go closer but now I am looking at my normal reflection. What I saw must have just been my sleepy eyes playing tricks on me. I somewhat preferred the smudged image though. My hair is a mess and I need a coffee to get rid of my tired eyes and my lips and chin are red and blotchy and a huge part of me is very glad Will left early and didn't see me looking like this, though I smile thinking how he is the cause of some of it. It is certainly not the peaceful vision he had of me while I was asleep according to his sketch though.

As I turn from the mirror and head towards the stairs I hear a click and a creak. I look back and realise the spare room door has opened again. It unsettles me but I must not have shut it properly. As I walk back I hear the music box still playing but then it stops abruptly, not slowing down into silence as I would expect but as if someone has closed the lid. I pause on the landing feeling foolishly spooked and stare at the half opened door. I shake my head telling myself I need to stop imagining things to be more sinister than they really are. After everything it may be understandable but I have never been the kind of girl who jumps at her own shadow and I am determined not to become that way now. I take a step towards the room and hear the box ring out once more but this time it sounds different. At first I do not understand what I am hearing and then I realise it is playing backwards, the tune distorted, the scratching noise of the drum turning more noticeable between each note.

This is what I heard in the woods. That was why I didn't recognise the melody.

But how can it be? And how can a music box play backwards?

It is old I tell myself, probably much older than me and played with by many other children through the decades. The mechanism has some strange fault I cannot imagine right now but talk to anyone who knows about these things and they will explain it. That it sounds like what I heard in the woods is just my mind playing tricks on me. Still trying to make sense of what happened all those days ago. It has to be.

I do not want to go any nearer to the room but I need to shut the door. I need to not hear the music any longer. I tentatively retrace my steps along the landing, reaching out my hand as far as possible so that I don't have to go any closer than necessary to the source of the unnatural sound. I quickly clasp the knob and slam the door shut making sure it is definitely closed this time but the music still reaches me as if I were standing right beside the box with the porcelain dolls holding their silent vigil around it, consuming me in its twisted lullaby. And I look to my reflection in the mirror once more and again it is out of focus, blurred, almost flickering like a bad TV signal and I want to blink to make it right but I can't stop staring at it and at the darkness swirling around my image which is nothing like the hallway I am now standing in. But then it is, then it feels as if the darkness has seeped from the glass and is now surrounding me. I am encased in it, drowning in it.

Lost.

***

It is getting dark before I am aware again. I am on my couch and there is mail in my hand. It's a letter about the upcoming inquest into Nathan's death I am to attend. I am dreading it but it seems unlikely it will be ruled as anything other than suicide, especially after it was discovered all his embezzlement was about to be revealed and he would lose everything and probably end up in jail.

I know he didn't come up to the roof to commit suicide of course. I know he had other ideas about getting away with what he was doing. Only one person had found him out at that point and if that person could be silenced he would have nothing to worry about, maybe even make it look as if they had been the crooked one in the company if it came to it. All he needed to do was just be more careful in the future. Not sleep with the wrong people who would have no problem revealing what he was really like.

I shudder, the more I think about the old me, the me back in London, the more alien she becomes to me. I remember finding Nathan attractive, having fun with him even and yet I am not sure why I was on the roof that day. Was it because I was struggling with revealing Nathan for his crimes because I had feelings for him or was it because I was struggling with what would be the best way to handle things for me? How could I benefit the most out of this discovery?

How can I not know exactly what I was thinking back then? Maybe I just don't want to admit what sort of person I'd really become back in the city.

I put down the letter. I am still shaking with the fear from not knowing what I have done in the time between shutting the spare room door and now. I realise that I am dressed, not still in my robe from this morning. I must have had a shower, picked out clothes and gone to collect the mail from the little box on my gate at least so why can I remember none of it? I gaze around the room trying to see any other clues as to how I might have spent my day. Everything is in its place. I pick my book up from the coffee table but the marker is still where I left it the day before. I go to the kitchen passing the green man on the wall who leers at me and I wonder what he has watched me do today. I look around the kitchen. A coffee cup sits on the counter, remnants of cream and granules still clinging to its side as if it has not long been empty. I am sure it was not there from last night, but there is little else of note until I open the fridge and find that it has been stocked. There is milk, beer and wine and cheese which I must have bought today.

Unless Will did? It is possible he would have gone out and bought food and drink for later but it seems highly unlikely and that would not explain where my day has gone. I suddenly have a terrible thought and run to find my phone. I glance around the room trying to see where I could have left it. It is not on the coffee table. I frantically feel around between the cushions on the sofa but it has not fallen down them. I run upstairs and see it in the bedroom sat neatly on the night stand. I grab it, pressing the button to turn it on and am thankful to see that it is still Saturday. It tells me the date is the 22nd of February and the time is 5.15pm. At least I have not lost more than a day, only a few hours. It is small consolation though.

I am going to have to find a doctor. Should I tell Will about me losing another day? I don't want to. He is the one thing holding me together right now. The one good thing in my life. If I tell him about the blackouts would he understand? Would he hang around to find out just how crazy I am? It's not something I really want to bring up after one night together. It is more of a six months into the relationship kind of conversation. Or six years.

Maybe it is not a conversation I will have to worry about at all if I can just figure out what is causing all this. It all started when I came here. Maybe there is something weird about the house. I've heard something about granite in the area being the cause of health issues. Could it be that? Is that even the kind of health issue it causes? Is the house on some kind of gas line or natural leak that's causing me to lose hours, days? I would actually like to think so. It may make it harder to sell but it's a better thought than the one that I am losing my mind.

I leave the phone on the nightstand and go back downstairs just as the front door opens making me jump but then I see that it is Will. He peers his head around the corner, still clearly not confident enough to just walk in yet.

'Hey,' he grins at me and I smile back at him which he must read as a kind of permission as he relaxes and walks in closing the door behind him.

'Hey,' I reply, pleased for the momentary distraction keeping my thoughts from spiralling any further.

'I'm sorry I had to go early this morning. I didn't want to.'

'That's OK, you had a job to do.'

'Did you find the note I left you?'

'I did.' I forget my stress for a moment as I remember it. 'I liked the picture you drew of me.'

He drops his head looking a little embarrassed as he walks over to me.

'I got inspired,' he shrugs, slipping his arms around my waist.

'You've got real talent.'

'I don't know about that.' He studies my face for a minute as if tracing the contours once more in his mind as he did on the paper, then kisses my forehead and walks to the fridge. Confident enough to help himself to a drink I see. Maybe he was the one who put it all in there. 'I'm glad you found it anyway. I was worried earlier today as I saw you and you blanked me.'

'You saw me?' I realise I sound too surprised.

'Yes in the village. I called to you but you didn't even look up.'

'Oh, I'm sorry.' I don't know what else to say. I want to ask him what I looked like. Was I in a trance? Was I confused? How confused could I be when I maybe managed to do a grocery shop?

'Don't worry about it. I've been in my own little fantasy world today too.' He glances at me, his eyes twinkling and his mouth twisted into a knowing grin as he retrieves a beer from the fridge and walks back over to me.

'Yeah, I have been kind of zoned out all day,' I admit and it does not seem far from the truth.

'I didn't know you smoked,' he says casually, a little hiss coming from the can as he pulls it open before taking a swig of its contents. The statement seems so random it throws me for a moment.

'I gave up,' is all I can think of to say.

'But not today?' There is something accusatory in his voice but I don't think for one minute it is because he is anti smoking. It is as if he is trying to work something out about me and it's troubling him. Maybe he already knows something is wrong and he's just waiting for me to admit it. I am not ready to yet though.

'No,' I say quickly. 'I was worried who I would see in the village so forgive me for feeling the need for something to calm my nerves.' I sound irritated and defensive which is not how I want to seem.

'I'm sorry,' he says, putting the can down and placing his hands on my arms reassuringly. 'I didn't mean to come across all judgey. Just didn't know you smoked. That's all.'

My mind turns to the note in the cigarette packet I had found a few days ago. Have I left myself another one? Has the trauma of what happened given me a split personality? Is that even a thing that can happen? If I'm not already crazy I'm driving myself that way. I need to speak to my therapist. She was the one who thought it was a good idea I came here and took as long as I needed. I doubt she thought I was going to start falling apart quite as badly as this. I need to call her right now.

'Um Will, I just need to lie down for a bit. I can feel a migraine coming on. Do you mind?' I move back from him.

'No,' he looks concerned. 'Do you want me to go?'

'No, no you're fine. I just don't think I'm going to be good company if I don't try and shake it now. A quick nap and I should be alright.'

'OK. You want me to start dinner?'

'You cook?'

'Depends if you have pasta and sauce?' he grins, that same boyish smile I remembered in my dream this morning and I want so much to forget my worries and forget dinner and just grab him and take him up to my bed with me. But my fears aren't going anywhere so instead I say.

'In the cupboard. Pretty sure there's some mince in the freezer too if you're feeling adventurous.'

'Got it,' he says, opening the cupboard as I retreat upstairs.

I shut the door to the bedroom and grab my phone finding my therapist's number and quickly press call. I listen to it ring out five times which seems like forever and I panic she's not going to answer. It's Saturday night, she's probably preparing dinner with her perfect husband and perfect kids in her perfect sane life, but then she does.

'Elena? Are you OK? I've been worried about you.'

'Honestly I don't know.'

'What's been happening?'

And so I tell her about the losing days, about the trouble I've been having with some of the people in the village but I skim the details of that as I am not ready to tell her about the councillors who have died or relive exactly what happened last night. Instead I tell her of the discoveries in my past, of the sister I never knew I had. And the whole time I am staring at the little bottle of pills beside the bed. Did I take one last night? Should I have? I know I considered it when I got out of the shower before Will became the only thing on my mind but I'm sure I didn't. I can't blame my blackout on them this time.

She listens patiently and I can imagine her taking notes and even if I could see her I know I would never be able to tell exactly what she was thinking, how concerned she really was or how much she really believed.

'Elena you say you are losing time, blackouts? Can you think of anything that triggers this?'

'No, this morning I was fine, happy even despite everything.' I think about telling her about the music box playing backwards and the strange reflection I saw in the mirror but can't bring myself to describe any of it and I manage to convince myself that it is not important enough to mention. The fact is I've lost a day. A faulty music box won't have caused that, and the image I saw of myself seems a trivial point, just my imagination perhaps warning me that I was about to blackout again. 'I was just about to go downstairs to get some breakfast. Next thing I know it is early evening and I am sat with a letter about the inquest.'

'And you say you've stopped taking the antidepressants.'

'Yes.' I glance at the bottle they are in again and for some reason the admission makes me feel worse. I can't pretend that perhaps I took one last night. I know I didn't and that they are not the problem. It is me. The problem is me. 'I didn't want to get dependant on them.'

'That's fair enough.' She takes a beat and again I think of her ticking off some box, considering her diagnosis. 'And in that case don't you think the letter may be what triggered the blackout? It was stressful. In all your sessions with me what is clear is that if something is traumatic your brain seems to shut down. Forget about everything. You could never remember the exact details of what happened with Nathan and you say you could never remember your childhood before. We didn't know the reason for this. Now you find out you had a sister who died. Your mother clearly didn't want to talk about her or for you to even remember her. Just like you she apparently wanted to shut out anything bad or unpleasant. It seems you may have adopted her coping mechanism.'

'So how can I un-adopt it?' I ask. 'And surely if I block out everything stressful why do I remember those men chasing me?'

'How did you get away again?'

'What?'

'From the men, how did you get away?'

'I told you, I hid and they went. I don't know where.'

'They just gave up looking for you?'

'Yes.'

She is silent for a moment.

'Elena I think you need to come back to London. We need a proper session. Find out what's going on. This splitting from reality concerns me.'

'Splitting from reality? I'm losing time I'm not delusional!'

Figures in lakes, bells chiming, distorted reflections. Aren't I?

'Like I said, I think we need a proper session. This is not something I can easily do over the phone. Can I schedule you in next week?'

'Yes,' I say but I do not want to go back just yet and I don't feel a proper session is going to do me any good though what was I expecting? I know now what I was hoping; that she would tell me everything I was experiencing was understandable and nothing to worry about. I never imagined her to make me doubt that even the things I know to be real are part of some fantasy. Those men chased me last night and the girl I saw…

The girl I saw, was she real? She seemed it but then she didn't. And then she vanished.

'So I have a cancellation next Friday, 10am. Can you make it then?' I forget for a moment to answer. 'Elena?'

'Um, yes, sorry. Friday is fine.'

'Good. I'll see you then.'

I finish the call and there is a knock on the door that startles me. I chuck the phone on the bed as Will comes into the bedroom holding some tea.

'Hey, I thought you might like a drink. Make you feel better,' he smiles setting the cup on the bedside table. I stare at it, light blue with little white daisies sprayed across it, wishing that its contents could really make me feel better. 'And,' Will continues sitting down on the bed beside me, his hands neatly on his lap, legs together as if he is scared to touch me. Even after last night there is still a shyness about him. 'I was thinking about how you just gave me the old headache excuse and I read somewhere that contrary to popular belief the thing that headaches are often used to avoid actually is very good for curing them.'

I can't help but smile at him as he says the words to his clasped hands then coyly looks up at me, desire glinting in his eyes and a grin playing on his lips and I cannot resist him. Maybe he is right and he is the best distraction from all that is happening.

'Is that so?' I question, amused and doing my best to push all other concerns from my mind. 'And was this in an official medical journal?'

He shrugs, 'probably.' He places one hand on my thigh and then slips off the bed so that he is kneeling before me.

'Aren't you supposed to be making dinner?' I look down at him as he runs his hands up my legs, easing them apart and moving in between them.

'Probably,' he murmurs without looking at me and instead busying himself with the belt on my jeans, slipping it from its loops before sliding his hands beneath my thighs and lifting them up and towards him so that I have no choice but to lean back on the bed. And as he throws my jeans to the floor I try and think of some witty protest, something to make things not quite so easy for him, to make him work just a little bit harder but his lips are suddenly on me teasing and exploring and it is harder to care about the lost hours or my therapist or anything that is happening beyond this room. All that matters is Will. All that matters is now.

***

The moonlight filters through the curtains bathing everything in blue and calm and I lie with my head on his chest feeling safe finally; safe from those men; safe from my past; safe from myself, at least for a while. I stroke my fingers across his alabaster skin and he gently kisses my head and laces his fingers with my own.

'I missed you,' he whispers and I know he is talking about my leaving when I was a child.

'I'm back now.'

He sighs as if he doesn't quite believe it still.

'Why didn't I ever get the chance to say goodbye to you?' I ask.

He is silent for a minute. 'You just didn't.'

'I'm sorry,'

'It wasn't your fault.' There is a bitterness in his tone and he squeezes my hand more tightly as if he is afraid I will go away again. I will have to of course at some point. I will have to return to London but right now I don't want to think about that so instead I say.

'You've got me back for good now.'

'Have I?'

'Yes.'

We lay in silence for a while lost in our own thoughts, his hand gently stroking through my hair, his fingers twisting in the strands.

'Elena, do you believe in the occult?'

The question is so random I laugh. 'I've never given it much thought. I take it you do though.'

'Why do you say that?'

'Um, the whole tragic vampire look,' I tease giving him a playful bite to his chest.

'Ow,' he laughs. 'I'm not sure if that's a compliment or not.'

'Compliment,' I shrug. 'Kind of.'

'Ok, but I'm being serious. How much do you know about witchcraft, the spirit world, all of that?'

'Um,' I frown wondering where this is going, 'not much.'

'Do you believe someone can come back from the dead?'

'What, like reincarnation?'

'No.' His hand stills on my hair, 'like possession.'

I almost laugh but as I look up at him, his face is so grave it stops me.

'No.' I shake my head. 'No I don't.'

I can't tell what he is thinking but he looks troubled as he searches my face for some kind of answer that I can't give him because I don't know what the question is and again I wonder if he is looking for my sister. That he wants to believe a part of her still lives on in me somehow. Am I just her replacement for him? Was it her he was so sad didn't say goodbye? We still haven't really talked about Elsbeth as every time I ask him about her he clams up.

'Do you?' I ask.

'No, no of course not, not really.' I wonder if his answer would have been different if mine had. 'It's just someone told me once they thought that if someone had died wrongly, before their time, that if their hold to life was strong enough they could return, that they could find a way back to their loved ones.'

'And you believed that?'

'No it's silly,' he laughs self-consciously. 'But it's a nice idea right?'

'I guess, I don't know. I doubt the person being possessed would be that happy.'

'No they wouldn't.'

The gravity in his voice troubles me so I roll over putting my legs on either side of him so I can look down at him and see if he is really being as serious about all this as he sounds. He manages a smile but I'm not convinced and I want to ask him who he would want to come back. Is it my sister? Is it someone else? The thought that he is thinking of anyone else right now makes me feel insanely jealous and I don't want to hear who it might be so instead I make light of it.

'Are you getting weird on me Malone?'

'Thought you liked weird?' he raises an eyebrow, whatever was troubling him seemingly forgotten. I'm reading way too much into this.

'In moderation.' I lean down and kiss him and for a while my insecurities are forgotten too.

Chapter 17

    Two days have passed since my inexplicable loss of time and the panic I felt because of it. Things feel better now. I feel better. Will has been with me almost constantly, helping me with the house, clearing all the brambles from the back garden, fixing the guttering. And when we are not doing chores we are chatting and laughing about all the memories I have had of us as children. He never volunteers his own memories though, wanting me to recall things on my own first and when I do he gets a look of wonder on his face as if he can't quite believe I finally remember the moments we shared while I wonder how I could have forgotten him at all. And I feel human again around him, I feel real. It's like I've been in a vacuum since December and he's released me. I can breathe again. I can be myself again. I tell myself now that my biggest worry is whether I should pay him for all the work he's been doing around the house considering it is how he makes his living but somehow offering him money feels wrong when we are so intimate. But if my mind strays onto the lost days, the men who wanted to hurt me, who perhaps still do, I focus back on this one simple problem. It is a stupid worry of course. I shall offer Will money. He will probably refuse and if he doesn't I won't for a minute be offended. There is actually no concern there at all but it is nice to believe, if only for a second, that is all I have to worry about.

    Now I sit at the kitchen table reading the local paper. There is an article about the three councilmen who died. Seems they were all original inhabitants of the village which, according to the paper, is becoming a less and less common thing. Times are changing. People move away to be nearer to the cities to find work and are replaced by families who have moved away from the cities to find peace. Holiday homes are more profitable than small holdings. Community is not as tight knit as it once was. From what I've experienced though I'm not sure I share that opinion.

I read how two of the men left family behind. The one I thought of as Punch had a wife, two adult daughters and a baby grandson. The barrel also, surprisingly, had a wife and a son at university. Geoffrey was the only one who had no surviving family. Apparently he lost his son in a boating accident several years ago which was subsequently followed by his wife's suicide. He'd made his life about the village after that, championing causes, arranging charity events. An upstanding citizen respected amongst all it seems though something about the article makes me think respected is not the same as liked.

Perhaps I don't hate them as I thought I did. I certainly wouldn't have wished the accident upon them, upon anyone. Everyone has their issues and problems. Poor Geoffrey certainly did. For some reason they took theirs out on me, because of some gossip from years ago that likely only they remember and they just made the mistake of sharing it with those horrible drunk men who would use any excuse to scare and hurt for sport. They weren't to know the extent their prejudices would affect me. They probably never even considered it. Bullies so often don't. It just made them feel better, more important, more in control perhaps. Maybe it was just like I am doing now; worrying about Will being offended at me offering him money and making that the issue rather than dealing with the bigger problems which are much harder to solve if they can be fully solved at all.

Just then my phone rings out. My heart sinks for a moment as I see my therapist's number and I consider not answering it for a second in fear that she will force my real problems upon me once more and make it harder to deny them but I take a deep breath and hit accept.

'Elena, how are you feeling?'

'Um, good actually. No more episodes. Things seem more settled now. I'm more settled.' I realise how forced my voice sounds as if I am desperate to convince her I am fine and then that in turn will allow me to convince myself. I wonder if she hears it too.

'Good, that's good. I think you should still come in on Friday but I wanted to tell you that after your call I've been doing some research.'

'Oh.'

'Have you been staying off the antidepressants?'

'Yes.'

'And can you remember the last time you took one?'

I think back to my second night in the cottage. I remember looking out of the bedroom window and imagining what might be still waiting in the woods for me, still not able to fully convince myself nothing had risen from the lake, then the panic attack I had felt coming on as I thought about the dark waters, the slime hiding whatever lay beneath.

'Tuesday,' I say. 'Almost a week ago.'

'Right, OK,' I imagine her making some note on a yellow pad in front of her. 'I've been talking to some of my colleagues and they confirmed that, in some rare cases, the tablets you are on can cause blackouts and even hallucinations. The antidepressants are the most likely cause of what you've been experiencing. Like I say it is rare but it happens and perhaps more so than the pharmaceutical company who supplies them would like to admit.'

'But I had the last blackout on Saturday. I told you this. It can't be the tablets.' I know now I am sounding irritated but that's because I am. Why is she calling me wasting my time when we've already discussed this?

'But your particular tablets have a half life of four to six days. They could still be what caused your episode. You lost a day initially after taking one then some hours after that while the drug was still in your system.'

I want to believe what she is saying but I've already considered these possibilities and they just seemed desperate excuses to explain away what happened, the real reason far more complex and sinister.

'Maybe,' I agree though I am still not fully convinced.

'Also have you been drinking alcohol while taking them?'

'Yes,' I admit and feel a bit like an underage girl caught in her parent's liquor cabinet.

'Right.' Again I imagine a comment being scribbled on the yellow note pad. 'Elena you know that is not advisable.'

'I've drunk since I started taking them though, just the odd glass here and there, nothing extreme but I've always been fine. It's only since being here that I've started to be affected.'

'Drugs can be unpredictable. Just because you got away with drinking with them a few times doesn't mean you can always. You came off the pills when you arrived there and then decided to take them again. All kinds of things can cause side effects where they didn't before, Elena.'

'I didn't realise. I never thought they would do that to me, if I had…'

'Many people don't. When you're in that sort of pain or have the kind of levels of anxiety which you suffered, you just want to take something to make you feel better and ignore the small print that very occasionally it might just make you feel worse.'

I feel suddenly very stupid. Being told all I've experienced has been entirely my fault, just a product of drinking and medication is a huge relief of course, but it was not only I who suffered from my ignorance. I think about the missing girl, the police time I have wasted, the parents who I must have caused unspeakable grief to.

'I don't always read all the terms and conditions when updating iTunes either,' I try and make light of what I've just been told but my words lack mirth.

'Who does? Look, don't worry about it, I didn't mean to come across judgemental.'

No, I think. I'm sure there is something in a therapist's contract which tells them they mustn't be judgemental or at least hide it when they inevitably are. Sometimes in our sessions I wish she had been, rather than nodding and agreeing with all I said. Sometimes I wish she had told me that she thought Nathan's death had been my fault; that he should be sitting on her couch instead of me. I wish she had yelled at me and told me that I was evil and a murderer and that I should hate myself for all that happened. I would have defended myself then perhaps as I don't believe it. Not really. It is just what I think others believe because I can't fully explain what happened on the roof that night. I can't really explain why Nathan died. Now I think of the missing girl's mother, the expression she had when she looked at me after the questioning, as if she wanted to make me hurt just as I had unwittingly hurt her in believing that her child was dead and once more I wish I was being yelled at and punished. It is what I deserve surely for being so careless.

'It doesn't say explicitly not to drink, just that it's inadvisable,' my therapist continues calmly just as I wish she wouldn't. 'Believe me I have many patients who think a glass of wine to wash their medication down is part of the prescription but clearly in your case that is not a good idea. If you come in on Friday and feel you still want something on hand I'll prescribe another type and see how you get on with them.'

'I don't think I want any more pills. I don't truly think I need them. I actually feel more like myself than I have done in as long as I can remember. Even my childhood memories are coming back. And I haven't even had a panic attack for the last few days. Besides I like knowing what I'm feeling is real again, not feeling so numb. And after what I've been through with these last pills I really don't think I want to touch anything like them again.'

'I understand and I'm pleased to hear you're feeling better. You certainly sound more positive than you did the other night.'

'I am.'

'Good. Well I'll see you Friday but any problems before then and you call me.'

'I will, and thank you.' I hang up the phone. Despite still feeling bad that I may have been able to avoid some of the stress I have been under, some of the stress I have caused others, the relief I'm feeling is immeasurable. I am not losing my mind. I am finally getting it back.

I go upstairs to find Will. He is not in my bedroom as I had thought but in the spare room which I have avoided since the incident with the music box. Now I realise all of that was just chemicals, acid and alkaline reacting with my brain cells, changing my perceptions. Nothing played backwards, doors didn't open by themselves and reflections didn't inexplicably alter. Everything was just a waking dream, a waking nightmare. I wonder even if the rabbit on the floor was real now or just my addled brain remembering what Geoffrey had told me about the little girl taking her favourite toy with her when she went missing and then distorting that information into some weird hallucination mixed up with my irrational fear of the lake. I never asked Will if he moved it. I'm not about to now. I think I know the answer. Nothing was there. The councilmen never snuck into my house, never planted anything in the bedroom only to have it retrieved later to give back to some girl in order for her to hold it when she met me on the pathway home the other night. It is only now I realise how ridiculous that idea was and I am pleased that I never mentioned it to my therapist. Anyway, it is over now. Time to move on, time to forget about it.

 I walk into the room and see Will by the doll shelf, holding the music box.

 'Hey, what you doing?' I ask him.

 'I remember getting you this,' he says quietly, caressing it in his hands just as I had two days ago.

 'This was from you?' I walk over to him leaning against his back and slipping my arms around his waist. I rest my chin on his shoulder and look down at the object trying to remember him giving it to me but despite feeling overwhelmingly fond of it no memory comes.

 'Yes, it was your birthday, the last one you spent here. I remember seeing it in the antique shop in the high street. I knew you'd love it so I ran home and checked all the money I had from washing cars and helping my dad to mow lawns. I was ten pounds short but the shopkeeper let me have it anyway.' His words catch in his throat and he rubs his eyes and although I can't see his face I am sure he is crying.

My birthday, I think, and also my sister's.

Involuntarily I step back from him.

'I thought it was my aunt's. I remember loving it though,' I say shakily. I don't know why I have this reaction when I think he may be thinking of her. I cannot truly be this insecure, this jealous.

Will nods and places the box back on the shelf and I see his hand quickly swipe at his eyes again.

'You did.' His voice is barely more than a whisper.

'Will, why did we never keep in touch? I was only in London. It's not like I'd left the country.'

'It wasn't that simple.'

'Why not?'

He places his hands on the music box again, his fingers stroking against it, lost in thoughts and I don't think he's ever going to answer.

'I did try to find you once,' he finally admits, a finger tracing the contours of the embossed little girl, sliding across her face, across the ribbons in her hair.

'And what happened?'

'The person I found wasn't you.' He pushes the box back on the shelf and turns to face me, his eyes blue pools of pain and I don't know what is causing it.

'You've found me now.' My words sound feeble. Has he really found who he was looking for? Did he never come looking for me before because he knew I wasn't Elsbeth? He knew he could never find her again?

He smiles and the fervour in his eyes burns away the remnants of tears and hurt and his fingers gently touch my face as they had just touched the little girl's on the music box, caressing my cheek before sweeping my hair back as I look up at him.

'I know.' Just two words but they are definite. Secure. Not as if he is secretly wishing I was my sister. Everything is going to be fine. No more hallucinations and losing time and no more jealousy for those who are lost. I shall remember my sister in good time. I shall remember everything from my childhood and in the same way I shall learn to put away the memories of Nathan and all that happened on the roof. None of that was my fault either. The inquest will prove as much. My life will go on and for whatever reason my sister's life will not and in realising this I feel very guilty about how selfish I have been. Worried about how Will feels about me, whether he misses her. She died. She doesn't get a second chance. I do. Maybe I don't deserve it but I get one and I am not going to waste it.

Chapter 18

I am on the beach and I do not know how I got here. I do not even know what time it is exactly but the sky is dull and grey and a couple of surfers silhouetted against the horizon play at the back of the breakers and I feel the freshness of dawn. The ocean breeze whips my hair away from my face and a curl of smoke wisps up from the cigarette between my fingers and I can taste the nicotine in my mouth and I can hear the screams of children. At first they alarm me but then I realise they are not real screams, they are not coming from the silhouettes in the distance but are echoes of another memory but this one makes my head hurt when I try and catch hold of it. This is one that I fear.

I try to remember how I got here but cannot. Did I sleepwalk? I don't think so. I am wearing jeans, a thick cream jumper; boots. Would I have known to put these on even in dreams? I cannot imagine it. The cigarette burns down onto my fingers and I cry out and drop it into the sand. I stamp on it quickly, wanting to crush it into oblivion remembering Will asking me about my smoking. Remembering this is something that now happens when I am not myself.

Since the call from the therapist I have been fine. I flushed the remaining antidepressants down the toilet. I counted the hours since I last took one so that I was sure every last trace of them was out of my system. I walked through the village. Talked to shopkeepers, people in the park, passed the time about the weather, problems with the economy; the price of milk. No one threatened me, no one blamed me for anything I may or may not have done. No traumas, no drugs, nothing to cause another episode. And I have never seen any of the men who chased me through the woods again.

So I have no idea how I came to this beach or what may have triggered another blackout.

I look out to the ocean for answers, ominous and dark as the slate which surrounds it. I watch as it swells and undulates, rolling towards me before arcing into waves, spray flung and fizzing from their peaks as they finally break, crashing down, roaring in my head. But once broken their power dissipates until nothing more than white foamy lines race to the sand, frothing and bubbling as they are driven to shore but weak in comparison to what they were only moments before.

Something happened here.

The sky is lightening and I see one of the surfers fall behind a wave.

And I hear the screams again.

It is not just those of children but those of adults. I can feel their presences as they run past me, see their shadows dash into the surf, be enveloped by it, crying out to those who are out of their reach and who are being carried even further from them. The noise is deafening and thunderous and piercing all at once and I close my eyes in an effort to shut it out. I don't want to know this. I don't want to relive it. And then all is quiet again and I am still standing in the same spot except now the surf has pooled around my feet making me jump back and I almost drop the cigarette packet clutched in my hand. I look at it and realise I have crushed its contents gripping it so tightly as another memory ripped through me, but only half a memory for I have no understanding of what I just experienced or indeed of what it was telling me that I experienced in the past.

I look at the crumpled packet in my hand, the lid open revealing only two cigarettes when the last time I looked, days before, the pack had been almost full.

And I see there is another note.

I stare at the neatly folded paper, stuffed down where another me knew I would find it. I am not sure I want to look at it. Will it tell me how I came here? Will it explain more lost hours? And how many hours have I lost? The last thing I remember was falling asleep last night, Will beside me. Was it last night though? Am I about to find out that it was two nights ago; more?

There is no point in torturing myself any longer. Whatever is on the note cannot be worse than not knowing. I pull it from the box, my finger still throbbing from its burn, and carefully open it.

There are three words written neatly upon it in my handwriting.

Don't trust Will.

Chapter 19

Someone is still playing games with me. I am starting to believe that not all was my imagination, not all was the fault of tablets which had never affected me badly until I got here. I wanted so much to believe my therapist's theory of what was happening to me and it seemed so plausible but deep down I knew it wasn't. I tried to believe, even convinced myself for a while but ultimately there is more going on here than just a bad trip on pills and alcohol. I didn't imagine all the people who threatened me and I didn't imagine that there is some reason from my past which is why they want me gone. They were desperate enough to terrorise and chase me, to lie in wait for me outside my house that night, to think that they had the right and authority to demand me to leave, to do whatever they liked to me. Now I am sure that they were also desperate enough to sneak into my house and place a child's toy there, I didn't just imagine it as I had hoped. So what other lengths would they go to? Why should it surprise me that I am losing time? How much would it take for someone to slip something into my drink? To try and make me run back to London fearing for my sanity? To not even think twice about what it might do to me? This has nothing to do with antidepressants and drinking, this is something else.

I don't think I need my therapist's appointment anymore. I'm not sure what good it will do when what I really need is a toxicology report. The thought sickens me. What is worse is the thought of who has had access to my drinks that could make this happen, who has had access to my house, who is there every time something happens to me. There is only one person and I have already written a note to myself warning me about him in some moment of lucidity I cannot remember. But why? Why would he be doing any of this to me?

As I stumble back along the coastal path my legs feel heavy, my whole body is numb. Only my mind feels alive and hectic, so many thoughts rushing through it as if there is not enough room for them and they are crammed so tight fighting for attention that my skull feels as though it is about to crack with the pressure.

I think mostly of Will. How he looks at me, how he touches me and how I feel about him. Surely he could never hurt me. Surely what I've been feeling is real and I haven't just fallen for a lie. But then I remember all the times I've seen pain in his eyes, all the times I have wondered if he was wishing I was Elsbeth. Are my worst fears true? Does he pretend that I am my sister? Am I just some consolation prize to him? Or did I do something to her? Is it because of me she is dead? Is that what he is punishing me for now? Does he perhaps have good reason to? But then I remember all the times he has told me that nothing was my fault. All the times that he has tried to protect me. He seemed so sincere. Though exactly what wasn't my fault he has never made clear and I have been too afraid to ask. Is he the person I think he is? This loving and caring boy from my past, or is this just what I am telling myself because I am so vulnerable right now? Because he has been a wonderful distraction from everything that has happened, that is happening and for once in my life when it came to men my guard was down. I barely put up a fight with him, just let him right in, let myself fall for him all over again just like I did when I was five years old and still believed in fairytales.

I don't believe in fairytales anymore.

As I reach home the house is silent and I realise he has gone to work already. I am thankful. I remove my wet and sandy boots as I get inside the door and then pull the bolt across it, leaning my back against the solid wood keeping the world out and taking deep breaths but they do little to make me feel better this time. I am not just having a random panic attack. My fears are real and hiding away in the cottage does not make me feel any safer as it has done before. I cannot escape the sickness in my stomach or the throbbing in my head. I cannot escape anything. I ran down here, leaving all that happened behind me in London and yet wherever I go it seems there are more people who want to hurt me, who blame me for things I don't understand.

I look up at the stairs and remember the first memory I had when I got here. Of being dragged down them, of my aunt even wanting to be rid of me. I was sure it couldn't have been a real memory back then before events started to suggest otherwise. Though something about it still seems distant, not vivid as those I have had since, maybe because I don't want to face that it actually happened though that seems a redundant hope when people from the village have given me every reason to believe that it did. What is wrong with me that people hate me so much? What did I do?

I stare at the stairs but no more of the memory comes to me, no more explanation of what it could have been about. I push myself away from the front door and stagger into the kitchen noticing my phone on the side. I grab it and quickly check to see today's date. Wednesday 26th. What I thought it was. I have only lost maybe a few hours but that somehow seems small consolation. I put the phone down looking around the kitchen, trying to remember something of this morning and I see the tea caddy sat innocently on the worktop by the kettle. It is full of the herbal tea Will keeps making me.

Did he make me a cup this morning? Is he poisoning me? Could that be even possible or is this just more paranoia on my part? Just another sign I am spiralling towards a total breakdown. The tea was in the house before he ever got here wasn't it? And it's not as if I black out every time I drink it. Was he still here when I left this morning? Did he notice something was different about me? Did he care?

I go over to the tin picking it up and removing the lid. I sniff at the contents but all it smells of is herbs and the earthy scent of green tea and I can feel tears of frustration pricking at my eyes as I launch it across the room, crying out as the tin clatters on the ground, leaves scattering across the floor. I grab at the kitchen counter, choking back sobs, bracing myself for the panic attack that I am sure will come but it does not. Instead there is just despair and emptiness. I have no one left to trust. No one left to love. I have no one. I am entirely alone.

I can't stay here.

Chapter 20

I spend the rest of the morning in the village and nobody pays me any mind not that I would likely notice if they did. I feel as if I am in a vacuum again. I have to stay busy though. It is the only way to stop my world caving in on itself.

I walk past the church and look up at the spire, black and ominous against a grey sky. Maybe my sister's whereabouts have been right under my nose. If she was buried here it won't tell me how she died or why her existence was kept from me but it may tell me the when. Anything to keep my mind off Will and what part he might have had to play in the week's past events.

I pass through the little wrought iron gate, which hangs open today, and into the graveyard. Though I have taken only a few steps from the main high street it seems more peaceful here. More sheltered I suppose, making it feel as if even the wind and trees have grown hushed in reverence for the dead. I walk up the tiny path which winds its way to the stone archway sheltering the gothic church door, the only sound gravel crunching beneath my feet. The gravestones are like soldiers standing to attention either side of me as I walk amongst them; a general inspecting her troops. Most are very old and weathered, channels forming on the stone from generations of sea air and heavy rains, decaying the script chiselled upon them which offers names of those who died at least a century ago. Usually I would be fascinated by the old names, the dates, making me wonder what their lives would have been like, how different everything must have been at the time their birth and death was recorded on the stone but so little else to tell us of their lives. Today it frustrates me that there seem to be no modern stones at all. I believe my aunt was buried here. I must find out. If she is I should arrange for a head stone. She doesn't deserve to be forgotten. No one does.

Then one stone does catch my attention and for a moment I believe I have found what I am looking for before common sense kicks in and I realise the grave I am looking at is clearly much older than the one I am seeking and then I see the dates which confirm this. It is for a young girl but not as young as my sister when she died, not a child. It is for an Elizabeth Reynolds; 1876 to 1897. I wonder if she was any relation. Reynolds is certainly not a Cornish name and I am not sure when my family moved here or why. I walk up to the stone, off the path and onto the spongy ground and I reach out wanting to touch the words, wanting the stone to tell me more about who it is memorialising. As my fingers are about to graze the lettering though, a bell rings out, mournful and sombre and then another and I realise there is a service at the church. People start to emerge all in black, heads low, clearly mourners. I feel like a trespasser all of a sudden and I do not want to encroach on their grief so I hurry back down the path and out of the gate before I am seen. There is nothing for me in that church yard. Just dead ends and I suddenly realise how true that expression is.

I still do not want to return to the cottage so I have a coffee in the tiny café and find myself watching the lady brewing it very carefully. She probably thinks that I have OCD or something and am waiting for her to make it wrongly in some tiny way. I make a conscious effort to look away from her, staring out the window at the quiet street outside, shiny still from last night's rain, the occasional car flashing by with a hiss of spray from the gutter but otherwise there is little sign of life. I am overly grateful to the waitress when she brings the coffee to the table feeling stupidly guilty and paranoid that I was waiting for her to do something to it. It's not as if everyone in this village has been unkind. Far from it. It is just that a few can sometimes make it feel that way.

I place my laptop on the table and log into the free Wi-Fi with the password I can see written by the counter hoping I can lose myself in research and not be just staring at the screen lost in my own thoughts. I need to focus, to feel I have some sort of control and am able to take steps to at least work out something about my life right now. I go straight to the local paper's website. I look for an archive section but I can see none but there is a search box. My fractured memories put me at about eight when I must have left here. I had lost more of my childhood than I had previously thought. My sister must have died about that time for I have no reason to believe she was ever in London with my mother and me. I tap in Elsbeth Reynolds. No results found flashes obstinately up on the screen. I suddenly wonder if we always went by the surname Reynolds. My mother's flight to London and eradicating of my sister's memory could easily suggest she may have wanted to change her name and cut all ties with this place. Reynolds is my mother's family name but would she have had us take our father's name originally? I can't imagine it but it is possible. My next stop will be to get a birth certificate though my gut feeling is that it will have father unknown on it and besides that will take time and right now I want immediate answers. I tap in simply Elsbeth. It can't be that common a name. A handful of obituaries come up and one article about a bake sale. None helpful and also I realise no results before 2005. A small local paper is unlikely to have the manpower to archive every edition on line very far back. My next stop will be the library. I look at the little cursor still blinking in the search box waiting for me to tell it what to do next. My fingers feel numb as I tap in the next name I have been putting off searching for though exactly what I am frightened I might find I have no idea.

William Malone. Search.

No results found.

I feel a mixture of relief and disappointment. While I am feeling brave perhaps I will Google him properly but first I click back to the home page of the paper and gasp, a chill running through me.

There is a photo of the man who first chased me the other night, the very drunken one who had shouted at me in the pub while his friends tried to calm him. His friends who I actually thought at the time to be better than him and then they turned out to be much, much worse. He just wanted to hurt me but what they wanted to do would have destroyed me. I shiver as his fleshy face smiles out from a grainy photo. He looks younger in the picture than when I saw him, tanned and shiny, and I can tell it was taken in some bar or club probably on the Med, probably on some lad's holiday. The enlarged pixels in the blurry image with the other members of the photo cropped out make him look like a victim of some sort and I realise that is just what he is. I skim down the article below the picture and read how his body washed up on the beach this morning.

The beach I was on.

It does not say what they think happened or how long he may have been in the ocean just that he had been missing for a few days. His estranged wife called the police when he failed to collect his two year old son at the weekend and she couldn't contact him. Apparently he never missed an opportunity to spend time with his little boy and she knew something must have happened to him.

I close the laptop unable to look at his face anymore.

People around me are dying. People I have wished would just disappear. How can I put this down to paranoia? Something is happening here but I have no idea what it is.

But I am losing time.

And I was on that very beach this morning. Did I find him? Is that why I then blacked out? Or did some part of me know that he would be there. Does the other me know exactly what happened?

Trusting Will seems the least of my worries all of a sudden. I am not sure that I trust myself.

I finish my coffee, deciding I need something stronger. It is nearly noon already. *The Lady of the Lake* will just be open. Sally has never been anything other than friendly and chatty and it should be quiet right now. She gives the impression she knows everything that goes on in this village. Maybe I should have asked her more about the people around here from the start. About Will. Even if she doesn't know anything it will be good to have a conversation with someone to stop my own thoughts spiralling out of control.

As I walk into the pub I find that I am right in thinking it would be quiet, Sally is the only person in there, busy lighting the fire in the main area before walking back behind the bar.

'Hello, haven't seen you in here for a couple of nights,' she greets me, 'What you having?'

'A pint of Korev please.' I take a seat at the bar.

'Haven't seen Will in here for a couple of nights either,' she grins as she pulls my pint, her bright eyes looking even more cheeky than usual.

I'm still not used to the small town ways of everyone knowing everyone's business but I know she means no harm. I want to ask her what she knows about him anyway and if she's fishing about how our relationship is going it won't seem an odd question.

'Oh, is that unusual?'

'He normally likes to have a drink in here after work.' She places the beer in front of me. 'I'm guessing he's been a bit distracted lately though.'

'Distracted? How?' I realise I am sounding desperate and jumpy and as if to confirm this I notice Sally frown a little but the knowing grin remains in place.

'Do I have to spell it out for you? I've seen the way he looks at you.'

'Oh.' I smile, tucking my hair behind my ear self-consciously and wishing this nagging doubt about him would just go away. I want so much to trust him, so much to be happy about what she is saying but how can I be?

'And I take it that it's mutual,' she probes.

'I don't know,' I try to sound natural. 'I'm not sure I'm ready to get involved with anyone at the moment, especially anyone that I don't really know.'

'Well how do you think you start to get to know people?' she says, seeming frustrated that I am spoiling her fantasy for us. Her slightly irritated tone tells me she thinks I am being silly for being over cautious and it makes me want to scream at her. To tell her exactly what has been happening. To ask her exactly how I can ever let myself trust anyone again. How can you ever get to know people if they don't truly want to be known? When I don't even know who I am right now? But it is not Sally I am angry with so I swallow down my own frustration and despair and instead say quietly.

'I suppose you're right.'

'Anyway, Will clearly wants to get to know you better and I'm glad to see it. He normally keeps himself to himself. I used to think he was a bit weird to be honest always dressed in black like he's allergic to a bit of colour but I guess he didn't have the best of childhoods.'

'Really? He didn't? Why?' I think of all the times I've remembered having with him lately, all the games we used to play together and how much he would make me laugh with his stupid stories and jokes. They don't seem to be memories of an unhappy child unless I was just too young to realise.

'Parents died in a car accident when he was ten apparently. Think that was when he started going off the rails a bit, getting into fights. Your aunt gave a lot of her time to him. I heard she even looked into adopting him but she weren't young or married and I don't know all the ins and outs but tisn't easy ever getting these things through.'

It takes me a moment to digest what she has just said and my mind claws at reasons he wouldn't have told me any of this. Maybe it's hard to talk about his parents, he's said little of the past, wanting me to remember it on my own and I have been so preoccupied with my own troubles maybe it just wasn't something he wanted to bring up. But why pretend he hardly knew my aunt? It makes no sense.

'I didn't know he was that close to her. I didn't even know his parents died,' I admit.

'Really?' the surprise in her voice is like a dagger to me confirming that it isn't right that I don't know this already. 'He'd visit her a lot, especially towards the end. Really helped her out when she got ill. He took her death pretty hard actually. Can't believe he wouldn't have told you any of that. I was guessing that was what initially brought the two of you together.'

I don't know what to say. I feel my stomach knot and my throat become thick and a throbbing starts behind my eyes but I will not give the impending tears permission to come especially as I do not know if there is a real reason for them yet. But why wouldn't he have mentioned any of this? He has always given the impression that he barely knew my aunt. If they were close why didn't he talk about her to me? I have told him I don't really remember her, that I hardly knew her but he never volunteered further information. All I can think about is how my aunt left everything to me when he was the one who visited her, who took care of her. She tried to be a mother to him and then left him with nothing. But why? Did he do something to make her leave him out of the will and if not, why leave everything to me when I clearly wasn't the only person in her life to leave her estate to?

'I didn't know any of that,' I say shakily and take a long sip of my drink trying to steady my racing mind and hoping Sally can't see she's rattled me though I know that it is obvious. The one thing which was keeping my doubts about Will from consuming me was that there was no real motive for him to be anything other than my friend. Now I have the perfect motive and the usual one; money, of course. I feel as if the floor has collapsed under me and I want to think of an excuse to leave as quickly as possible without letting Sally know anything is that wrong but my mind is numb and I feel as if I've been punched in the stomach and all I can do is pretend to drink more of my beer but my swollen throat makes it difficult to swallow.

'Well you ask him again about her. I'm guessing he's still cut up about her death. Maybe he just doesn't want to get into a conversation about it. You know what men are like.'

I nod and take another drink but I know I'm not fooling her into thinking that I am in any way alright about what she has just told me.

'Here, you heard about Duncan did you?' she changes the subject quickly and I am pleased for it.

'Duncan?'

'Man that was in here the other night shouting his mouth off about you. Well they found him this morning washed up down Treleath beach.'

I try and keep my voice from shaking. 'I saw that someone was found,' I say. 'It was online.'

'Don't know when it happened or how long he's been out there. Saw a woman in the Co-op, Rachel Uglow, lives out by the park you may have seen her around. Husband runs the fish and chip shop, got a gammy leg.'

I shake my head.

'Anyway, she told me she was down on the beach this morning with her dog about 8 O'clock and a section by the headland had all been cordoned off.'

8 O'clock. I was home by then. He must have been found just after I'd left the beach. I certainly didn't see or hear anything. Apart from the surfers the beach had been deserted. I wonder how the newspaper got the story up so quickly but then in this place news carries fast.

'The police were trying to keep it all hush hush about who it was,' Sally continues. 'But Rachel spoke to a few people who confirmed it were Duncan. I haven't seen him or his friends in the pub since that night you were in here actually and they was all pissed as farts. Not surprising they stayed clear of here for a while after I had a go at them, bet they went up the road to The Horseshoe. Bit out of the village but they probably thought that it would teach me a lesson, depriving me of some business and all that. They spend quite a lot in here but not like I missed their company. Anyway from what I hear another one of that lot, Tommy, hasn't turned up for work for three days either. I reckon now people are going to be asking a few more questions about that.'

'Do you think something has happened to all of them?' I frown hoping I sound casual enough, though what am I trying to hide? How pleased I am that one of them is dead? That I am hoping maybe the rest of them will wash up on the beach too? Are those thoughts really so bad after what they wanted to do to me? Maybe when I know a young boy has been left fatherless they are. But is it more than my thoughts I am trying to hide or is it the feeling that I am somehow responsible for their disappearance? But how can I be?

'Put it this way, they're all a bunch of twats. Amazing they haven't fallen off a cliff before now, amount they drink.' She walks out from behind the bar and starts to polish the tables. Despite myself her directness amuses me, snapping me out of the strange guilt I'm feeling but not distracting me enough to keep another thought creeping into my mind. Will didn't want me to go to the police about what happened that night and maybe he was right. It wouldn't have done any good and I would be called into questioning now and it would be another reason for the village to distrust me in the light of what has just happened. But did he know that? Did he know me reporting the attack would complicate matters later on? Was there something more to his concern than just knowing it would be my word against theirs? Those men disappeared that night and I don't know what happened to them but Will was there, just like he was there when the council members threatened me but he never told anyone that he was. He made sure people didn't know. I wondered why at the time but thought maybe he was just trying to protect me, not wanting to embarrass me by letting people know about the men telling me to leave. Now I wonder if he was more trying to protect himself.

But then Will didn't make a tree fall on a car and kill three people and nor did I. I am not thinking straight. Maybe it is time for me to go back to London. Is all this really worth my sanity? Coming here was supposed to make me feel better, to get away from it all and gain some perspective and instead everything is worse now so what exactly am I trying to prove by staying? Will certainly isn't the reason anymore not now I know that he's lied to me. The cottage is done pretty much and what isn't can be left undone. I'll call the agents later, hand in the key and get back to my apartment in Kentish Town. Back to normality or the nearest thing to it since everything that has happened to me there, but where nobody knows your business or cares for very long even if they do. And where Will can't manipulate me.

And I hear the children scream again, crying out for me to remember them but, before I can grasp any more of the shadowed images or the sensation and emotions I had on the beach earlier, a pain sweeps over me like a vice shutting down on my brain crushing the memory before it can surface.

There is something more here and a part of me feels I know exactly what it is but that part is buried so deep it feels impossible to retrieve though I cannot run from it. I need to know what is happening to me now and what happened to me back when I was a child before I can leave this place behind.

'Will is a good one though,' Sally interrupts my thoughts and it is clear she is still worried she has said something out of turn about him. 'He had his reasons for not mentioning stuff I'm sure. Don't you go thinking too much on it.'

If only it were that simple.

'Did you live in the village when Will's parents died?' I ask, keeping my voice light and conversational, not wanting Sally to feel bad for anything she has just told me.

'No I used to live in Barrowford about twenty minutes from here,' she informs me as she rubs at a particularly stubborn spot on one of the tables. 'Only bought the pub ten years ago. Just know what I get told by the locals.'

I want to ask her what the locals say about me but can't bring myself to and if she wasn't here until ten years ago I doubt there is any point in asking her about my sister. I also get the feeling if she had heard anything about me she probably would have flat out asked me about it. She certainly never seems backward in coming forward.

The door clatters open and a couple walk in, obviously tourists, all walking boots and waterproofs, distracting Sally as she instantly goes into tour guide mode, hurrying back behind the bar and making them feel as welcome as she did me on my first night here when I thought I had left all my problems behind.

I decide it is a good cue for me to leave. I need to think through everything I have just learnt and I'm not sure I can do that here with Sally watching me and worrying whether she has put doubts in my head about Will. I can't face sitting in the library now struggling through archives either, especially when I remember there are news paper clippings in the trunk in the attic which I never got around to looking through. Maybe all my answers are there. I certainly need to check that before thinking of handing everything over to an estate agent to deal with.

I finish my drink, leaving Sally talking to the walkers about all the places they should visit and a few places they shouldn't, and head back up the lane to the cottage. The wind has picked up again and the day is darker than it should be for the hour, another bout of heavy rain on its way no doubt. As I walk past the edge of the woods a crow takes flight startling me and as I look out into the trees I think I see a shadow watching me amongst them but I know that I am just scaring myself now, my imagination running understandably wild after everything. I still walk a little more quickly past the trees though and thoughts of the elfish faces back in the painting above the fireplace swim into my mind and I imagine them peering at me now from the roots and branches, watching with amusement. Waiting for what I am going to do next. And I feel relief as I get to my little gate and the apparent safety of my threshold.

But then I see Will's truck parked outside. He is here, waiting for me. I glance through the windows of the vehicle and see plastic sheeting crumpled in the back. It has a rusty red substance on it and there is sand on his floors and seats.

I shiver. But am I really thinking he could have done something to those men? No.

I am being ridiculous.

But something nags at me that I once knew a different Will from the one I know now and the one in my fragmented memories.

And the next memory comes but this one hurts like it is being driven by a nail back into my mind, into my soul.

I am on the beach, the same one from this morning. The tide is out and the damp sand stretches before me, vast and empty. Will is with me, older than in my previous memories, and I don't know what to say to him to make it right for there is nothing to say. I have never known him so silent and although I know I am not responsible for his pain I feel guilty all the same. Guilty for not being able to take it on as my own, to take the burden away from him and make him whole again, but however hard I wish I could, I know that I cannot. And I want to tell him this but for the first time ever I am scared to speak to him as I feel there is a part of him which does see me as somehow responsible for his pain and one wrong word could end our now fragile friendship. He has changed and I know he doesn't even want me here right now but I stay beside him anyway waiting for a glimpse of the old Will. Waiting for him to realise that there was nothing I could have done to change what happened, nothing I can do to make it right but if he will let me I just want to help him get through it, to somehow make things a little better though exactly how I do not know. So instead of speaking I stare at my feet as they move across the sand which is rippled and ridged from where the sea has claimed it only hours before and will do so again shortly, wiping away our footprints and any trace that we were once here.

I am remembering the aftermath of the death of his parents, of how utterly helpless I felt and how much it hurt me to see him grieving almost as if the grief were my own. This is a black memory and I do not want to see any more but my mind has opened once again and the events come flooding from my subconscious as real and vivid as if they had happened only yesterday and I am powerless to stop them.

I am waiting for Will to say something. Surely he will say something soon then I will know what to say back. Maybe just my being here will help him somehow. I know I cannot leave him alone. I have done so for several days thinking that was what he needed. Now it feels as if I abandoned him. I hope he doesn't think that. I hope he knows that I would do anything for him. That for the last few days I have thought of nothing but him. Perhaps that is what I should be saying but I am afraid if I try and tell him it will all come out wrong and sound stupid and make everything worse. Maybe we don't need words at all. Maybe this is enough for now. And I reach my hand out to his, my fingers softly grazing against his palm, inviting and he doesn't react for a minute but then his hand opens and moves slowly over my own about to take hold of it but he pulls away as a stone thuds down onto the sand in front of us, stopping us both in our tracks.

'What are you doing with her Will? Haven't you heard what people say about her?'

Three boys are standing about six feet away from us. I know them because they are all in Will's year at school but I always make sure to avoid them if I see them in the playground or around the shops in the village. There is nothing friendly about them and I've seen them pick on and beat up some of the boys in my year before, and steal from them. One, Sam, is covered in big orange freckles with ginger hair cut short making his head look square. Overweight, his flabby cheeks wobble as he shouts out at us. Peter stands beside him. He is taller, good looking even, with blue eyes and black lashes but not like Will's. Peter's eyes have no compassion in them, they are steely and cold. His black hair is slicked back making his face look more angular than ever, his cheekbones sharp like blades beneath his flesh. There is no softness to be found in him and his otherwise handsome features turn vicious and hard with his expression. And the third boy, Clive, is the smallest, skinny with a mouth always hanging open revealing teeth too big for it and gaps between them even bigger.

'Would have thought after what happened you'd have finally come to your senses, realised everything she touches is cursed.' It is Peter's turn to shout.

'Shut up Peter,' Will yells and I notice his voice crack as he does. I haven't seen him cry about his parents yet. I kept wishing he would but not now. Please not now. I don't want him to give these boys the satisfaction.

'Why Will? Don't you want to hear what your little girlfriend is?' Peter's voice is mocking. 'No wonder her Dad wanted nothing to do with her. Bet he took one look at her when she were born and ran a mile while he still could.'

'What you talking about Peter,' Sam smirks not taking his eyes from me as he speaks to his friend so that he can watch my reaction. 'Like her mother even ever knew who the father was.'

'Just leave us alone,' Will says weakly. He has no strength to stand up to these bullies, not now and I feel angry with myself that neither do I. I can't think of any come back, any way to make them stop their taunts so as Will tries to walk forward I go with him in silence but Clive throws another stone and this one strikes me on the arm. I cry out, clasping at where I have been hit and I can imagine the purple black bruise which will soon be spreading across my flesh and I bite back the tears as I see all three boys laugh.

'Did I say you could leave?' Peter takes a step forward still flanked by his lackeys. I am still so shocked by the pain that at first I don't react but Will does. He lunges at them but there are three of them and although he stands slightly taller than Clive and Sam he has never been a fighter.

'Maybe he's a witch too,' Clive jeers, spittle flying through the gaps in his teeth as Will goes towards him. 'Maybe he hated his parents and they both ended them.'

Will gets one punch in, shutting Clive's ugly mouth for a second and sending him staggering back, wide eyed as if surprised his taunts would get such a reaction but the other two boys are not surprised.

Sam grabs Will, pulling him back from Clive before he can get another punch in and spinning him around to face Peter who wastes no time in smashing one fist into Will's face then the other into his stomach making Will slump over in agony but Sam is still holding him, keeping him from falling to the ground and Peter hasn't finished yet. Peter is enjoying himself.

'Peter, no! Don't,' I cry out wanting to go forward but fear and knowledge that there is nothing I can do, that they will just swat me to the ground if I try, keep my feet routed firmly to the spot. I have to be cleverer than that. I have to think. Peter ignores my screams, instead he grabs hold of Will's face with one hand, his fingers digging into his cheeks forcing him to look up at him and I see the blood running thickly from Will's nose and his eye closed tightly, already beginning to swell.

'That wasn't a nice thing to do Will.' Will tries to struggle but Sam holds onto him tighter, pulling his arms further behind his back so that he is prone.

'I said leave us alone!' Will manages, spitting blood in Peter's face

Peter smiles and wipes at his chin, looking at the blood now on his fingers. Then his eyes darken and his smile is quickly replaced by a twisted grimace that speaks of pleasure in hate and he slams a fist into Will's stomach again. I know Will would never give these boys the satisfaction of hearing him cry out but the groan which rips its way out of him as the air is beaten from his body is the worst thing I have ever heard.

'Stop it. Please,' I scream, knowing that I am too weak to do anything, knowing that there are no adults around to run to and I cannot leave Will to find them even if there were.

I don't think Peter even hears my cry. I have already been forgotten. There is a more fun sport to be had now. He bounces on the balls of his feet a little as if he were sparring and as if his opponent actually had a chance of fighting back before hitting Will in the ribs as Clive laughs holding Will up as if he were nothing more now than a punching bag and I want it to stop now. I have to make it stop. And as I stare at the terrible scene in front of me it is as if time slows down and a shimmer for that is the only way I can describe it, ripples through the air around me. I close my eyes and then the seagulls come.

They are big and menacing, screeching as they approach and I feel the rush of their wings before opening my eyes as they swoop past me, so close they almost catch in my hair but they are not here for me. They fly towards the boys and I watch as at first Peter doesn't notice them *so intent is he in planning where next to inflict pain on Will but then one dives at him and I see blood appear on his cheek where the bird's beak has hit him. He staggers back, flailing his arms about in an attempt to stop the birds but they continue to dive at him. Two flap around Sam who has now let go of Will, finally letting him fall to the floor and curl up, fighting to get the air back in his lungs though I can tell every breath is torture. The birds ignore him, instead they squawk and peck at Sam as if he was no more than a piece of bread they are fighting over. He tries to swat them away always looking back at Will, intent to not let him get away just yet despite this rude interruption to the fun times they were having but another gull comes and through the hurricane of wings and cold black eyes I see blood running from beneath Sam's eye. Any higher and he would have been blinded and only now does he back away from Will and run from the scene, his friends forgotten and thoughts only to save himself. Clive just stands, unmoving with his mouth gaping open more than usual. No birds have gone near him but he is transfixed and terrified, the wet patch spreading across his trousers proving how much. Peter falls to his knees in his bid to get away as a final bird swoops down on him catching some of his now not so perfect hair in its talons and ripping it from his head. He stumbles back onto his feet and runs from the beach so fast I only just hear his shout back at me.*

   'Witch.'

   And I know what he says is true and now just one glance at Clive sends him scurrying away too.

   The birds soar off into the sky, their prey forgotten. Just normal sea birds as before, their minds turned to hunting for fish and scraps. And watching them I smile and a thought occurs to me that if the boys hadn't have run, hadn't have given up so quickly, how long would the gulls have attacked them for? How much damage would have been done? And another thought occurs to me that I don't care.

I go to Will. He is clutching his face and I try to help him up but he bats my hand away. I know he is angry but now there is something else. Now there is fear.

'Will let me help you,' I beg him.

'Don't touch me Elena.' His voice is thick with blood and he struggles to his feet, one hand holding his nose and his other arm around his ribs.

'Will, please,' I say, still trying to help him up but again he pushes me away.

'I said don't touch me Elena.' He manages to stand. 'What they said about you, it's true. People get hurt around you. People die around you.'

'Will, no. You don't believe that. I know you don't.'

'Don't I? What was that Elena? What just happened?' He staggers back from me his good eye wide, terrified. I shake my head feeling him slipping away from me and I can't explain what just happened. I can't make him understand when I don't understand myself.

'I don't know.'

'You do Elena. You caused it. You cause everything.' His face wrinkles in pain and I see the tears that he has denied for so long start to come, all the emotional agony outweighing the physical. 'I don't understand how but you do. You're a curse on this village just like everyone says you are. I tried not to see it, I tried to stick up for you but I can't anymore. Everyone is right and maybe, maybe if you weren't here bad things wouldn't happen. Maybe if...'

He stops, coughing and spitting blood onto the sand then looks at me his eyes cold, all the humour all the compassion that made me love him gone, replaced with pure pain and despair and hate. 'Maybe if you weren't here my parents would still be alive.'

'Will, no. I know you don't really think that.'

'Don't I? You're a curse Elena,' he chokes back his tears, his voice gaining timbre. 'A curse and I wish you would have died in that car instead of my parents. I wish that it was you who were dead and not them.'

I stare at him unable to speak for a moment. If Peter had just grabbed me and hit me ten times as hard as he had just hit Will it would not have hurt as much as what I am now hearing. I must be in a nightmare and I need to wake up. I need to wake up now.

'Will, don't say that. You don't mean it.' My voice comes out thin and scratchy. This is not my friend talking, it can't be. It is as if someone has replaced him. Someone is wearing Will's skin, someone cruel and hateful. He doesn't even look like Will anymore, his face swollen and ruined as it is.

'Yes I do. I don't want you anywhere near me Elena. I don't want anything to do with you.'

And I watch him stagger up the beach and the words have come as such a shock to me that I can't speak again until he is almost out of earshot.

'Will,' I cry after him but he does not even falter. He is gone.

Did I really cause what just happened? Is it true what they say about me? Is Will right to hate and fear me? I wanted magic in my life for so long does that mean that I finally have it? And does that make me evil as they say? Does that make me a curse on the village causing hurt to people who I love? No. Of course not. I would never harm anyone intentionally. Would I? But I wanted to hurt those *boys. I wanted to hurt them so badly and is that really so wrong when they wanted to hurt someone I loved? And then I think of the feelings I had tried to ignore as I watched the birds fly away. The feelings I didn't want to deal with because they raise the question which would confirm people's fears of me. The question I don't want to ask myself but now I don't have to as I know the answer already.*

Would I kill for Will?
Yes.

Chapter 21

'Will?' I call out as I walk through the door but the house is empty. He is not here as I had feared. I do not have to worry about confronting him yet. He must have come to find me on his lunch hour and just left his truck here and walked to wherever his next job was. Making his claim on what he thinks should be his property no doubt. And now even my memories have revealed we weren't always friends like I had believed, imagining we were some sort of star crossed childhood sweethearts finally together. Pathetic. That is not real life. That is some made for TV movie on one of those cheap cable channels where everyone is a bit too perfect; a story in one of my aunt's books up in the attic with the titles all written in flowery italics which I scoffed at her for even reading.

There was a time when he hated me. Did that ever change? It's the last memory I have of us as children. Was it just the grief of his parents' deaths talking or did he really mean what he said? Did we ever recover from that? Does he still blame me now somehow? Is that the real reason he never talks about our childhood? Never volunteers more than I tell him I've already remembered? Maybe he was glad I'd forgotten that day. It made it easier for him to infiltrate himself back into my life.

And what of Elsbeth? Is she who he really cared about? Who he really misses? Is that why I've blocked her out? Was I jealous of her? Did I do something to her because of that? And what really did happen that day on the beach? I remember feeling certain at the time that I had somehow caused the birds to behave that way but now I know that is ridiculous.

But what if it isn't? How much has to happen around me before I have to start believing that I am capable of things others are not. How much before I am as terrified of myself as some people in the village are of me. And if that is the case what did I do to Elsbeth? What did I do to my own sister? I don't want to remember but I know I must.

I waste no time going up into the attic and back to the trunk which has already offered up so many revelations to me. As I switch on the light, I look at it hunched across the room like a Pandora's box and I know, just like in the myth, that once I have discovered whatever truths it still holds I will never be able to put them back. I will be changed forever in ways I may deeply regret but this needs to be over now. I need to know my past.

Taking a deep breath I march over to my nemesis and kneel down before it, stroking my hand across the wood as the bare bulb lighting the room swings precariously again on its wire, caught in the draught I could not find the source of and casting shadows which sweep back and forth across the chipped white paint of the trunk. I lift the heavy lid, remembering the last time I did this I had thought I had always been an only child. I thought I had only lost memories, not a sister. How could that have been less than a week ago? It feels like a lifetime.

I heave out the albums I have already searched through from the chest and I am left looking at the few remaining papers strewn at the bottom. I notice my hand trembling as I lift them out and it makes me realise how truly terrified I am of the truths which lie in wait.

The first clipping I look at is surprisingly about Will's parents and I wonder how different things would be now if

I'd continued looking through the chest's contents all those days ago. My aunt had kept this for some reason like other people would keep articles about their kids in a show or some charity event, something they would want to have a memento of. Something they would be proud of. Why would anyone want a memento of this? There is a picture of a wrecked car smashed into a tree and I read how the roads had been slick with mud from farm traffic earlier in the day and that it was believed that Chris Malone had swerved to avoid a deer and lost control of the vehicle, killing both him and his wife, Laura, instantly.

Tears come to my eyes as I remember how Chris used to tease me and make me laugh. How Laura would ask me all sorts of questions only little girls would be interested in, so pleased Will's friendship with me had given her a chance to pretend she also had a daughter. It was so long ago and yet I feel the loss so strongly now, Will's loss. And however much I no longer trust him I hate that he had to go through this. He didn't deserve it. No one does.

I put the paper carefully on the floor beside me and reach for the next one. This is equally tragic. Why did my aunt keep such tragic cuttings? Why would she choose to remember such things?

Unless they weren't for her to remember.

Did my aunt disagree with my mother about never speaking to me about our lives here? We never came to visit her when we moved to London and my mother never spoke of her and a part of me remembers being happy about this. A part of me remembers feeling uncomfortable about Aunt Carol like she knew a truth about me that I did not want revealed. That I was terrified would be revealed.

Did she also think I caused all these things to happen? Was she as superstitious as everyone else in this village?

Did she try and tell my mother her beliefs and that's what caused us to leave here and why they never spoke again?

Again the memories of distrusting her seem so distant it is like trying to grab hold of smoke despite them being feelings I know I had about her from after we moved away. From a time I thought I remembered clearly and yet it is a time that seems to become hazier and hazier the longer I am here.

I start to read the article now in my hand hoping that it will provide some answers.

I see the date and it would place me at being around eight years old when it was written. Right about the time we moved to London. The light above me swings across the headline illuminating it so that it seems to jump out at me. "Four children die in boating accident". I shiver and my stomach churns. This will be the truth about what happened to my sister. Will told me that she drowned. This will be what I am so afraid of remembering, what I have blocked out years of my life to not have to deal with. I am convinced of it.

As I try to still my trembling hand and will my reluctant eyes to read, the dusty bulb above me swings away from the paper once more and I hear the whisper of the draught it is caught in and, as the light flickers and goes out, it sounds like the word 'no' hissed, extinguishing the bulb in its exhale as if it were not made from glass and wires but of wax and flame.

Only the dull light seeping from the open hatchway to the ladder below keeps me from being in total darkness. I could use this as an excuse to give up. To come back to this story another day but I cannot. This needs to end now. I fumble in my back pocket for my phone and swipe on the torch, trying to hold it steady above the paper in my hand.

The article is not about my sister. A mixture of relief and disappointment rushes though me and I don't know which I feel the most as I start to read about four boys who drowned. They were swept out to sea in a catamaran; there was a sudden riptide and only one boy survived.

William Malone.

And the memory that has been threatening to return since the beach this morning hits me so hard I drop the paper and have to put my hands onto the cold floor to steady me as I am sent back to a time I must have tried so hard and succeeded for so long to forget.

Will has been ignoring me since his parents died and after what happened on the beach that day with the gulls. He was the one person, or so I thought, who never believed the rest of the village when they said that I was weird, calling me a witch and a child of the devil just because a few strange things would happen around me. I am not evil. I don't understand the things that happen, they just do. Bullies get hurt, animals get healed. I can make no sense of it but I do feel the tingling which goes through me when it happens. My aunt tells me it is nothing to be afraid of, that I just have to learn to control it. She says that my mother wouldn't understand as she never had the gift and neither will Elsbeth for not everyone can be born special.

Special is not a word I like to be called. I want to be normal. I'm too old now to want or to believe in fairy magic like I used to. And I don't want my sister to hate me like she does because she feels I am different and because of that she thinks I get more attention than her, like attention is always a good thing. And I don't want to talk to my aunt about it anymore. Will is the only person who really knows me and now he is just like all the others. It is as if he blames me for his parents' deaths and all he does is hang around with Sam and Peter now and their gang. Boys who threw stones at me and pummelled him to the ground and now he is their friend. If they throw stones again will he stop them?

Will he join them?

I am starting to hate him. I tried to talk to him the other day but he told me to go away and as I turned back to walk to my house feeling the tears pricking my eyes, I saw Elsbeth smile.

I know she has always liked Will. It is the one thing we have in common except she had no interest in spending time with the both of us and as Will spent all his time with me that meant she was always on the outskirts, watching on, jealously waiting for her time when we would not be such good friends.

Now her time has come and I hate her for it and I hate him.

It is when we are at the beach that I see him again. It hurts to look at him now. Like looking at the sun; it promises light and warmth but get too close and it will burn you, look too long and it will blind you. And maybe I am blinded because I decide I have to try to talk to him again. I have to mend us somehow. Elsbeth actually encourages it. It is the first time in what seems like forever that she has been nice to me and so I approach him as he walks to the ocean where his friends are waiting in the small catamaran, two pushing it out into the water while the others sit on board fiddling with the sail.

'Will, please talk to me. It's OK if you don't want to talk about what happened with your parents I won't make you but I can't stand us not being friends.'

'Go away Elena,' he says and tries to carry on walking but I grab his arm.

'Will please. I know you didn't mean what you said the other day. I don't understand why you are being like this.' I hear jeers from the boys on the boat and see his cheeks flush and I know they are partly to blame for his reluctance to hear anything I have to say. But he is better than this surely, better than them. But then he proves that he is not.

'I said go away Elena,' and he pulls my hand from his arm, his fingers digging into me, and pushes me to the sand. 'I don't want anything to do with you anymore. Why can't you just accept that? Why are you so pathetic? Just leave me alone!' And his eyes that have always been filled with kindness towards me flash vicious and cruel and I know that his parents' deaths have changed him.

And I watch him join his friends as I struggle to my feet ignoring the pain in my hip where a rock had dug into it as I fell. He wades into the water and swings himself up onto the vessel, saying something to Peter who laughs and two of the boys on the boat shout something at me as they start to sail out over the waves but I can't hear exactly what because the wind whips their words from me and I am grateful for that. Still, even unheard words can hurt.

And I feel the tingle go through me but I breathe in and out, in and out just as my aunt has told me and the tingling stops and the catamaran continues smoothly out past the breakers.

And then I feel her hand slip into mine. Elsbeth. She is smiling, calm and serene but her eyes are hooded and dark as she joins me in looking out at the tiny vessel weighed down with the boys, struggling over another wave as they jostle with the sail and position themselves on the netting.

At first I am so happy that she has come to see if I am OK, to give me support when I need it. Maybe now I am not friends with Will she will not be so jealous and I will have my sister back. Maybe that is some consolation for losing him. But then the tingle returns, more than a tingle this time. It is as if a jolt of energy has gone through me so strong I cannot breathe and in that split second I see the catamaran flip and I hear the cries of the boys as they tumble into the sea. One cracks his head on the side of the vessel before falling limply into the water, not struggling like the others whose arms are flailing as if they are trying to grab the air to keep them from sinking down as the sudden rip tide, for that is what it must be, tries to claim them and take them forever into its depths. And I see them start to choke as the water floods their open mouths and they disappear beneath the waves.

I see Will disappear beneath the waves.

And I try to breathe in and out, in and out and calm myself but how can I when all the air has gone from in me and around me and now all I can feel is my sisters grip on my hand. I try to get free of it but she just squeezes tighter so it feels as if she may crush my bones, her finger nails digging into my flesh and I know she is still smiling and I watch as people run past me into the waves, out to the drowning boys and all I can think of is Will. He cannot drown. He cannot. I don't care how he has treated me lately. It is Will. I cannot exist without him. I will not.

I am back in the attic, the light has come back on and is once again gently swinging on its wire and the newspaper article is crumpled on the floor beneath my hand as I crouch, fighting to get my breath back as if I am still in that moment, still watching the boys drown, still willing

Will to live. I snatch up the paper, screwing it up as tight as I can and throw it across the room.

People think I killed them just because I was there that day, that I killed them all. That I was somehow responsible then and that I am still responsible now for all that is happening. Every bad thing. That is why people want me to leave. But it is not true. How can it be? It is ridiculous. I was a child buying into the superstitious nonsense that was spread about her. The tingle I felt, the loss of air were all just shock of what I was witnessing; a boat getting into trouble; children caught in a sudden riptide. Nothing more.

I was just a child.

How could they, grown adults and even my aunt who should have known better, have done this to me? Made me believe I was a curse, that I could have somehow caused those boys' deaths. That I could have caused anything to happen?

But what if they were right?

I leave the attic, feeling drained and having to steady myself by putting my hand against the wall as I walk down the stairs. This is why I blocked everything out. This is what I was protecting myself from; the guilt over something that was not my fault, something that I could not have changed. The guilt that comes from wishing someone dead and that wish coming true.

It is a feeling that I am getting used to.

And my sister was there that day. I finally have a clear memory of her but it is a memory I do not want.

So I know everything now, the reason my mother never talked about our time here and the reason I readily forgot it too.

Except I don't know everything yet.

I still do not know how my sister died.

I do not want to remember. I already know. I will have been somehow responsible or have been made to feel responsible. However bad that last memory was my sister's death will be worse, of that I am sure.

Lost in my thoughts I don't realise anyone is in the house until I walk into the kitchen and Will is there. He has picked up the tea caddy I threw earlier and is sweeping up the tea leaves and putting them down the sink. I don't want him to do that. I wanted to keep them, take them somewhere and make sure that they were nothing more than tea leaves.

'Hey, what happened here?' he asks, eyes full of usual concern and I hate him for it. All the shock, all the pain from what I have just relived is swept away by one thought. That Will is the real reason I am hurting so much right now. He still blames me for everything that happened, the boat accident, my aunt leaving this house to me instead of him, maybe even for his parents' deaths, and now he is making me pay. Everything he has told me he felt about me, every time he made out that he cared about me has been a lie and I have played right into his hands. He wants me gone as much as those councilmen did, as much as those men who chased me did. And an awful thought enters my mind. Maybe none of those people cared if I stayed or not, maybe none of them really hated me or even knew who I was or what people had once said about me but Will did. Will remembered and it was Will who asked them to terrorize me. It was Will who told the councilmen to demand that I go back to London. It was Will who made me believe I was about to be raped and who had me chased through the woods. It is all starting to make perfect sense. Why he was here when the councillors threatened me, why the men from the pub just disappeared right before he showed up and I want to hurt him for it. I want to make him pay.

'I could ask you the same thing,' I try to keep my voice steady.

'Elena what's wrong?' He places the dustpan and brush on the counter and comes towards me but I step away from him.

'What are you doing here Will?' I feel my eyes moisten as I look at his confused expression and I ignore my gut telling me to trust him just because it would be so much easier and less painful to do so. It's too late for that.

'I just finished work early. I thought I'd come and...?'

'I mean what are you doing here in my life? What are you doing acting as if you're my friend, as if that is what we have always been?'

'Elena, we are friends of course we are. I'd hope more than that.'

I almost laugh, shaking my head. 'We are not friends Will, maybe once but not now and not even back when we were children. You hated me before I left here. You told me that. You told me you wished that I was dead. Do you still wish that? Do you still wish it was me who died all those years ago instead of your parents?' And the next words tumble out even though I don't want them to. 'Instead of Elsbeth?'

'Elsbeth? What? Elena what are you talking about?' His eyes flick away from me, bewildered, searching as if he is flipping through a rolodex of memories in his mind before he looks back at me. 'Look, if you're remembering what I think you are you know I didn't mean that. You must know I didn't. My parents had just died and I was only ten for god's sake.'

'Exactly! Your parents had just died. Do you realise that is the first time you have ever mentioned that to me.'

'It is?' He looks puzzled like he cannot understand why I am so angry about this and for a second I wonder if I am over reacting but then I think of everything else he has also failed to mention.

'It is,' I spit bitterly, 'and you never even thought to tell me that, even though you knew I didn't remember it. You never thought to tell me that it was my aunt who wanted to adopt you after they died. You never thought to tell me about how you looked after her while she was ill, how cut up you were about her death. None of it. Instead you acted as if you hardly knew her and I was wondering why. Why would you never have mentioned any of this? Why wouldn't you have let me know from the start how close you were to her, to a person I am trying so desperately hard to remember and then I realised. You didn't want me to know. You didn't want me to know because then I might figure out what you were up to. I might figure out that you were just here to worm your way in and gain my confidence, trying to get your hands on the inheritance that you think should be rightfully yours. Trying to get your hands on this house. '

'I'm not,' he says feebly. 'I never would, Ele..'

'Then why didn't you tell me any of this Will?! Why did I have to hear it all from a stranger?'

'Elena, I'm sorry. If I'd thought it was going to freak you out this much I would have said something. You've had so much going on though, you've been under so much stress I've never felt bringing up my parents' or your aunt's deaths were exactly great topics.'

'I have been under a lot of stress lately haven't I Will? And why exactly do you think that is?' I say steadily, my anger cooling to a simmering hate as I calculate exactly what he has done to me. 'Do you think maybe it was because you were trying to scare me, to make me feel as though I were losing my mind, hoping that I'd leave you to take care of everything and just disappear back to London? Do you think that could possibly be the reason?'

'Elena, what are you talking about?' He looks genuinely confused but this time I am not buying it.

'Don't pretend you don't know Will. How convenient that you taking care of everything was exactly what those councilmen suggested when they came round. What did you do? Offer to buy them a pint later on to thank them? No wonder you didn't want anyone knowing that the reason they were on that road when the tree fell was because they were at my house that night. Because you had told them to be there!'

'Elena this is crazy.' He comes towards me and for some reason this time I let him. 'I had nothing to do with those men threatening you. You can't honestly believe that I did and the other reason I didn't mention how close I was to your aunt was because I just thought you'd start asking about her and…'

'And what?' I feel myself weakening again. I want him to have a good explanation. I want him to tell me I have it all wrong. I want to believe him. I want to trust him so much but how can I?

'And I didn't feel I could talk about her with you. There are things, things I want to ask you. Things I want you to remember but I can't say them to you because I don't understand what's happening. I just know this is real.' He tries to touch my face but I flinch, stepping back. None of this is real.

'Don't.' I push his hand away, regaining my strength. 'I know the Elena you know right now might seem gullible and vulnerable and maybe I fell for all those lines initially but not anymore.'

Now it is Will's turn to take a step back. It is as if I have stung him. 'I don't think that, I…'

'Oh please Will I know that is exactly what you think. I was an easy mark. I bet you couldn't believe your luck when I didn't have any memories of you, of anything. All that wanting me to remember things on my own, at my own pace crap, that was just because it made it easier for you not to have to pretend you were sorry about how you treated me. You didn't have to explain away how much you hated me back then or make up some reason why you don't still feel that way now because I didn't remember any of it.'

'Elena I don't hate you. I never hated you. I lov..'

'Don't,' I hold up a finger. 'don't you dare say it. Don't you dare insult my intelligence by thinking I'm going to buy into some empty words of how much you care about me.'

'They're not empty, they're the truth!' The hurt expression is gone, replaced by angry determination. He knows his hold on me is slipping away and I don't want to let him speak. I don't want him to say anything which will make this any harder.

'They're not the truth Will. They're just not. You hated me before the boating accident and I don't think for one moment you weren't with the rest of them when I was chased out of this village because of what happened to your friends. Because of what everyone thought I did. Because those boys all died but somehow Will Malone lived and I wish he hadn't,' I try to sound strong but my voice cracks and I have to swallow back the tears. 'I really wish he hadn't.' I regret the words as soon as I say them. I don't mean them, not really. It is the eight year old in me retaliating to all the things he said to me at that time, but they are out now and I can't take them back and if they just make him leave I don't want to.

'Chased you out of the village?'

'Yes, I remember that too. Being dragged down the stairs by my mother, made to take the back way out to avoid some lynch mob who wanted me gone. Something tells me if you weren't with them you wished you had been.'

Suddenly he looks afraid, truly afraid. I expected anger or denial but his face is ashen like he has just seen a ghost and his next words make me wonder if he has.

'Elsbeth?' he asks as if that is my name and not the name of my dead sister.

'What about her?'

He swallows, taking another step towards me.

'She keeps coming back doesn't she?'

What?

'Will I don't know what you are talking about or what game you are playing but I need you to leave, now!'

'I'm not going anywhere Elena.'

'No you really are,' my words come out weaker than I want and I don't know whether I am about to have a panic attack or a reaction to something more sinister but the room seems to have gone darker than it was a second ago and black patches play on the corners of my vision.

'Elena I don't know what's happening to you but you have to let me help you.' He reaches out to me but I manage to shake off the feeling so that my vision clears and I step back towards the door.

'Don't come near me Will,' I say but before I can say any more a wave of pain washes over me. I double over feeling as if I may be sick and this time the black spots dance in front of my eyes so that for a moment all I can see is darkness and it is as though they are pressing into my skull but I blink them away, kneading the heels of my hands into my temples. I can't deal with this now. I can't show Will anymore weakness than I already have.

'Elena what's the matter? You have to tell me what's happening to you.' Again he comes towards me and I hold out my hand to keep him away but as I do, I glance in the mirror and see the same blurred reflection of myself as I saw the time on the landing just before I lost hours of my life. It is still like a bad replica of me, faded and hazy as if the mirror is particularly dirty or uneven like that which you'd find at a fairground attraction. And Will turns to see what I am looking at and it is not so much that I see him tense but that I can sense it and I can tell that he sees it too. I am sure of it. It is not just my imagination and he looks shaken as he turns back to me as if he is expecting to see my image as it looks in the glass. Does he really know what I am seeing or is this just part of the act?

'She's getting stronger isn't she,' his voice trembles, his face as pale and as hollow as the other me, the blurred and distorted version who seems half erased in the mirror and I think of my aunt's painting hidden behind a sheet in the attic, of the figure by the lake fading into nothing. Is that figure supposed to be me?

I manage to stand up. The pain subsiding. I look in the mirror again and see my normal reflection.

'Is she getting stronger Elena?' This time his voice is authoritative, demanding, like I am a distracted child who needs to pay attention.

'Who?' My confusion over what just happened makes me forget I do not want to enter into a conversation with him. I do not want to play whatever his next game is.

'Elsbeth.'

For some reason the way he says the name chills me.

'My sister died. That's what you told me so how could she possibly be getting stronger? Just stop lying to me Will!'

'Your sister didn't die.' The words come out quickly as if, had he thought about them for any longer than necessary they would never have been said. I stare at him, searching his face for some truth to this revelation. Is he lying to me now or is my sister really alive? Did something else happen to her that she could no longer live with us? Was something wrong with her that meant my mother couldn't cope? Is she in a home somewhere because of it? Or was there some other reason? Could she be leading a normal life, her real family forgotten? Is that why I couldn't find a gravestone or any clue about when she might have died or why? I have no proof of anything that I am being told. I no longer know what or who to believe. It is as if all the air has been sucked out of the room, a million questions running through my head.

'Will if my sister is still alive you need to tell me where she is.'

'I can't.'

'Why not?' I scream.

'Because I don't understand it myself!' he yells back but then becomes calm again, his eyes sincere and intense as he takes a step towards me. 'Your aunt did though. That's what I could never tell you. That's what I wanted to avoid telling you because I don't see how it can be true but your aunt told me you would come back. She said you were strong, stronger than Elsbeth and you would come back as soon as you saw your chance. You would take back what Elsbeth had taken from you.'

Now I realise I am never going to get any truth from him. He is never going to admit to the game he is playing and he is never going to stop playing it.

'I can't listen to any more of this Will,' I shake my head, opening the door for him to leave.

'Elena please, you have to listen.' He slams his hand on the door shutting it again, his arm blocking me and forcing me up against the wall. 'Your aunt left you all this because somehow she knew you'd return. She was sick towards the end, really sick but the one thing she was sure of was that you had made it. Just like she knew you would. But she knew you needed to come back here to fully understand. And that's when she died. She told me things were finally going to be right and she could rest now.' Tears are welling in his eyes. 'I didn't believe her, I never believed her and then I saw you.' The words catch in his throat. 'Then I saw you.'

For a moment I am overwhelmed by the pain in his eyes, the longing, but only for a moment. I am done with theatrics and I am too tired to work out what story he is spinning me now. There is no point even to try and make sense of it. I just want him gone before I have to hear any more lies.

'Will you need to leave now,' I say as calmly as possible. His face is so close to mine I have to stare down at the floor to say the words. I can't look at him anymore.

'Elena I am not leaving you. You're not safe.'

'Damn right I'm not safe!' I scream pushing him out the way and moving from the door, distancing myself from him. 'I haven't been safe since I let you in this house. Oh god since I let you into my bed. How could I have been so stupid?'

'Elena listen to me. It's not me you need to be afraid of. It's her.'

'Who? Who's 'her'? My not so dead sister?' I almost laugh. 'My aunt?' I am on the brink of hysteria and I feel if I start to cry I am never going to stop. 'Are you going to tell me that she's alive too?' I have to get him out of my house. I try to push him to the door. I can't take any more of this.

'Elena you have to remember everything. If you remember you can fight her. You have to remember who you really are. Please.'

I have no idea what he is talking about. I can't argue with this craziness. I can't believe how desperate he is for this house. That he can't just admit he's been found out.

'Please Will just leave me alone.' I shove him harder but he grabs my wrists and plants his feet and I cannot move him.

'No, not until you remember,' his face is resolute. Why is he reacting like this? What is he so desperate for me to remember? What did I do to him?

'What? Seeing you nearly drown? Seeing your friends drown? There was nothing I could have done about it, Will. Nothing! Why are you punishing me now for it?'

'Punishing you? I'm not punishing you for anything,' he lets my wrists drop, his face crumpled and full of remorse as he staggers back, crushed and weary. 'How can you even think that?'

'How can I not?'

He turns away from me his head hung low as if he is searching the floor for an explanation, struggling with what he is about to say, what he is about to admit. My heart is thundering. I can't take any more hurt. He turns back, running his hands through his hair before they reach out to me open palmed as if he is showing me he has nothing to hide. 'I know how I treated you after my parents died and I was dreading when that would come back to you but I knew it had to just like everything else has to. It has to Elena. You can't hide from it anymore. And I know what happened to my friends but that wasn't you Elena. That wasn't you.'

I can feel tears fall down my cheeks despite myself. I don't want to cry in front of him.

'Please, please just leave me alone,' I sob. He looks up at me, tears are streaming down his face now and he shakes his head slowly.

'I can't. Not until you remember.'

'I've remembered everything I have to. Just go away!' I shriek, wiping my hands across my face which is slick with tears and clawing my hair back, clutching at my head in frustration and I can feel the pain in my temples begin to build again.

'No you haven't,' he shouts back grabbing onto my shoulders and shaking me.

'Then what, Will? What? Just tell me! What is so important that I remember?!'

'That your sister didn't die.' His eyes stare into mine, huge and wild. 'You did.'

Chapter 22

And I see her standing in the mirror, the darker eyes than mine, the jealousy and pain and greed all written on her face and I remember. I remember how jealous she was of everything that I did or had, jealous of my relationship with my aunt, jealous every time our mother would praise me for the smallest of things and most of all jealous of my friendship with Will. I remember how she told me that he was waiting for me in the woods that day in late summer when holidays were nearly over and the warm golden days were coming to an end. That he wanted to apologise for all the horrible things he had said, for the way he'd been treating me lately and that he didn't blame me for what had happened to his friends. He wanted to make sure I knew that. And I remember following her to the lake and wondering where he was and scanning the trees waiting for him to emerge and make everything right between us again. And then I remember feeling her hands hard against my back, shoving me forward and the sharp sudden cold of the lake enveloping me and how I couldn't swim which was strange because I could swim. I had my 400 metres badge but it was as if the lake were dragging me into it just like the ocean had dragged those boys under. And that was when I realised I was not the one responsible for what had happened to Will's friends and nor was it a sudden rip tide which could have been avoided if only they had known what to do. Because they would have known. They had grown up by the sea, swimming and sailing and knowing the dangers. And I realised in that moment that it was not only me who could make things happen as my aunt thought, as I had thought. Elsbeth could too.

I'd felt the energy go through me like light and stars cutting though the blackness of that day and I realise now that was why Will lived. It wasn't my hate of those boys that made them drown it was hers. It just meant I couldn't save them because I didn't really want to. I only wanted to save Will. I am not sure if she really meant to kill them either. I am not sure she is truly evil but she knows that I know that's what happened now and she fears me just like everyone else does but for a very different reason. But I will never tell. Surely she knows that. It will be our secret forever and I want to tell her that but I am sinking down so fast and I know I should be able to save myself just like I saved Will but her terror of being found out is so strong as is her hate and it is as if it consumes everything. And I cannot focus with my lungs filling with the green slimy water. They are burning in my chest and I open my mouth trying to gasp for air which isn't there and the lake takes the last of my breath and then all is blackness…

And I am above the woods looking down at my sister who is sobbing and muddy and I hear my name shouted and I try to call back but I can't but she does. She answers to my name. Elena. And she runs to my mother and flings her arms around her and tells her that it is Elsbeth who is in the lake. It is Elsbeth who has drowned. And I cannot listen to my mother's cries and I try to block them out and time loses all meaning.

The days grow shorter. The leaves turn from emerald to amber then fall lifeless upon the lake creating tiny ripples in its surface so calm now as if nothing bad ever happened here. And I cannot feel the cold but I see the ice which comes freezing them in place, creating frost which glimmers like diamonds along their veins before all melts, and they are just left dead and dull as before. And as new buds sprout on the branches above, the dead leaves wither into dust below. And the new buds flourish, warmed by the sun, and leaves unfurl from branches before being swept away by the wind and then all loses life again, all fades and perishes once more. And I do not know for how long I watch this cycle. I do not know how long I remain at the place of my death.

And then one day I feel a pull of energy and I shut my eyes and I let it take me and it feels as if I am hurtling through time and space, soft thick air rippling around me. Then it stops and I open my eyes and I can see myself again. Well not quite me. I am taller, my face slimmer, without the chubby baby look and I realise it is not me for my body no longer exists; It is mush; it is bones and maggots and decay. This is my sister I am looking at now, my sister living her life as if nothing happened. As if she were me.

She sits in her bedroom at a small white desk looking at schoolbooks, doing homework and I crave the tedium for it is real, it is to be a normal child growing up, working towards a future which I will never have. So I watch and as much as I hate her I pretend that I am her, just as she has pretended she is me.

I have friends, I go to parties. I stress about what Fiona said about my shoes and I feel joy when we are best friends again. I dread exams and dance recitals and get excited about sleepovers and cinema trips and then boys. I try to feel her first crush on some boy called Toby as if it were my own but it is not my own. My own was years ago now but it still feels as real and fresh as it did then.

I go through her heartbreak and rejection and for a while I forget to hate her and I do not envy her pain as much and yet I still envy it for to feel it is to be alive. And so it goes on. I am there for her first cigarette; first drink; first drunken one night stand at some party where Fiona had gone off with a boy she liked and so to drown out the pain two thirds of a bottle of whiskey was downed and then another boy saw his opportunity. I live it all, trying desperately to feel what she is feeling but it is all a lie, just as her life is a lie and everything I feel is a shadow of her emotions and there is no real joy, no real love and no real agony or despair, no real anything.

That is, not until she turns nineteen and he walks into the pub she often drinks at, Will Malone all in black, not the colourful shirts and over sized jeans his mother used to put him in. Where his hair was once dark brown and messy now it too is black and straight but still falling over his eyes. He smiles at my sister and for the first time in forever I feel real pain, real longing and for the first time I wonder if not feeling anything is really worse than this ripping now in my chest. He is still alive and he has grown and I have not, although in my mind I am nineteen and my feelings for him have equally matured.

He talks to my sister, his voice gentle and persuasive and I wonder if they'll mention me but they do not. It is like I don't exist. I suppose I don't, not anymore, but like I never existed. I can understand my sister denying my ever being alive but Will?

But then I remember it is not me they are choosing to forget. It is Elsbeth. Will thinks he has found me. Surely he will realise. Surely we knew each other better than this? That the things he is asking my sister if she remembers and she is saying she can't or she remembers them wrongly, are things which I would never forget. Never!

But he must think I abandoned him after my sister's supposed death and that I chose to forget all that he meant to me. After all he had abandoned me after his parents' deaths and it has been eleven years since I died. Since the village got rid of the child who scared them all so much.

And I want to scream at him as I see him laugh with her, reach out and touch her hand, gently stroke it, telling her how much he missed her and how sorry he was for everything. All the things he was supposed to say to me at the lake that day. To me! Why does he believe her? Why does he not see? Why? She can't take him from me. She can't! She can't! Please...

I don't remember much after watching her take him back to her student accommodation. The pain and jealousy and final acceptance that I am no more was too overwhelming. I know how she felt when he left though. I remember her one all consuming thought.

He knows.

And the thought made me feel stronger because I hadn't been totally forgotten. I did mean something to Will and he knew I wasn't the girl he'd just spent the night with. That I was more, that we had a connection that no one else could ever know or try to replace, that even though my sister had managed to fool our own mother, she could not fool my Will. He would never forget who I truly was. And for a moment I felt as if I was no longer watching her from a distance or pretending that I was seeing life through her eyes. I was there, in the room with her and she looked at me and I felt as if I was standing where the mirror normally was and I was looking back at her and she touched her face as if she were seeing something wrong with the reflection and then I was back on the outside again, looking at a life which could never be mine.

It is not until she is on the roof years later and thinks she is going to die that I get my chance again. It is as if a part of her has given up as she watches the man come towards her with the hammer. She has accepted this would be her end and her grip on life becomes a little weaker for she can see no way out but my grip on life does not. Mine becomes stronger. She is my one connection to living, to existing and I can't let that end. Not yet. Not like this.

And then I am on the roof and I don't know how I got here, I don't know how this happened. I don't know what's happening. Where is Elsbeth? Why is she not here too? And I feel the cold, which I had forgotten could sting and hurt, the icy wind billowing around me feeling like daggers running me through and I am shaking so much, gasping in air as if I had forgotten how to breathe. And then I notice the man now coming towards me and I see his anger and hate for my sister.

No. Not for my sister. Now it is for me.

And I want him to end.

I brace myself for what is about to happen, pushing myself up against the barrier and closing my eyes, expecting that at any moment I will feel the hammer crashing into my skull. That I will experience death all over again but that this time it will be all consuming. It will be total darkness. There will be no light to seek out, no life I can cling to. There must be a way out of this. There has to be.

There will be.

And I hear the hammer drop to the floor and the clatter of it makes me open my eyes in time to see him flinging himself over the safety barrier I am gripping so tightly to as if that was all he ever came up here to do.

And I watch as he falls to his death.

And I forget who I am. I forget that I died too. And my memories are replaced by hers except I have always been Elena, I never killed my sister for I did not have one and I do not remember my best friend Will, for to remember him is too painful for words.

Chapter 23

I am still on the roof but now it is different. It is not the day Nathan died. I am not even sure if it is day or if time even exists in this place. Snow still drifts intermittently through the air and all is in fog but there is no sound of the streets below, no lights blinking from the Shard. There is nothing. I am nothing.

She stands in front of me.

Elsbeth.

We are wearing the same clothes, the ones I put on this morning that I know I am wearing now, somewhere, as Will cradles me in his arms praying that I come back, realising that I am not breathing and feeling desperately for a pulse. I feel his tears fall against my skin but here they are as snowflakes though they warm instead of chill me.

'You took my life,' I say to her.

'And you tried to take mine.' Her eyes bore into me, dark and soulless, her hair lies lank around her face and I have the same feeling of the fear I had when I looked at her picture back in the attic. I didn't understand it then but now I do. Now I know exactly which child I was in those photos and why just the image of her filled me with dread.

'What did I ever do to you Elsbeth? We were sisters, twins.'

'We were.'

'Then why?'

'Because I had to.' Her words are definite, cold and the complete lack of remorse in them takes me aback.

'You didn't,' I shake my head. 'I wouldn't have told. You didn't mean to do what you did to those boys.'

'Didn't I?' The question doesn't seem rhetorical. I feel she is waiting for me to answer, wondering herself what happened that day.

'No,' I say though I don't quite believe it.

'So you didn't wish they would just disappear either? You didn't want them out of your life?'

'I didn't want to kill them. They were children Elsbeth.'

'So were we.'

'That makes no difference. I still didn't want them dead.'

'Didn't you?'

'No.'

'I don't believe you.'

I look down at the ground, grey and cold, the mist swirling upon it and remember how I felt when the birds had attacked those same boys, remembering the power which had surged through me and how I had liked it but I refuse to admit that I am anything like her.

'See,' she says as if she knows what I am thinking. Her voice oozes a calm authority. 'Everyone wishes ill on someone in their lives. Only difference is most people don't have the ability to make it happen. They have a chance to consider their options too, consider the consequences and those who would also be affected, the innocents who don't deserve to get hurt. And maybe that makes them reconsider their fantasies but maybe it doesn't. Maybe their wishes remain the same and they know how much better their lives would be without that person in the world but then they lack the opportunity so the person lives out their life whether they deserve to or not.' She shrugs. 'That is just the way it is every single day. They can't stop what they want or what they think any more than we can stop what we are capable of. Do you really think I am worse than anybody else?'

'Is that what you tell yourself? Is that how you ease your conscience for killing your own sister, for killing me?'

I see her lips turn down slightly, a flicker of regret flashes across her face and she has to look away from me, her confidence shaken for a moment and I feel her thoughts. She knew that I would never tell; knew that no one would believe me if I did but I made it harder for her to deny what she had done. Easier if no one knew the truth at all, for those who talked of curses and witches never really knew if what they were saying was true, perhaps never really believed it, but I did. I knew exactly what happened and I made it real and she couldn't face me because of it and then she couldn't face herself so she answered to my name when our mother came looking for us in the woods. She didn't want to end me. She wanted to end what she had done.

'Like I said, I did what I had to.' Her voice is gravelly, determined and I see her shake off any guilt she may have had, her confidence returning. Just how I have wrestled with my feelings about what happened to Nathan I know in the same way a sharper emotion than guilt pierces through her conscience and however sorry she is for what she did she would not have changed it.

'I was your sister,' I say though I do not think it matters to her anymore.

'And yet the only person who you really cared about was Will.'

'That's not true.' But again I can sense her thoughts. That is how she feels it was. It was not me she was jealous of, it was Will. He had taken her sister from her. That is how she sees it and that was why she didn't care if he drowned that day.

'Really? Isn't it? Did you ever even know I could do the same things that you could? Did anybody bother to even notice?'

'How could I have known Elsbeth? You shut me out. You shut everyone out!'

'No you shut me out!' she yells, her veil of calm slipping for a moment and I see her eyes become glassy but then she regains composure as quickly as she lost it. 'I could have told you to keep quiet about what we were capable of. I was five and I realised it but you were too stupid to even think about the consequences or to even realise you were different and when you finally figured it out people were already beginning to fear you. You got the blame for anything that happened. Bad things happen that's just the way of it but isn't it easier to have someone to blame? Will's parents weren't your fault, neither were half the things that happened in that village and they weren't mine either though sometimes it felt that way. They came for me and Mum you know. After you died and they thought it was me who had drowned, thought you'd finally killed your own flesh and blood and we had to get out before they practically broke the door down. I wasn't sorry though. I needed to get away from that witch of an aunt. She knew I wasn't you just like Will did when we met up again.' She tilts her head as she studies me. 'I took his virginity before he realised though you know. I think he'd been saving himself just for you. How sweet. Did you see that when you were waiting for your chance to steal my life from me? Did it hurt you to be on the outside for once just like I was for the eight years I had to share this earth with you?'

I try to ignore how much her words hurt me, pushing the thought of her and Will from my mind and blinking back the tears which come from thinking of him touching her still believing she were me, thinking of him making love to her, but I cannot hide the pain they cause. Nothing can be hidden in this place.

Her lips twist into an unpleasant smile. 'So you did see it.'

I can't bring myself to answer her and I know there is no need to. She already knows. I want to find the good in her but I can't. Not now. I turn away from her, looking down at the precipice behind me, at the swirling fog churning and hiding all that is below and I think about how I nearly came back after that night she had with Will. And I think about how it was only when she felt lost and frightened again that I got my chance to return once more. I look back at her. It feels colder now as if the wind has picked up, just like that day on the roof two months ago and yet the air is still. We cannot spend much longer here I am certain. 'If you had the same strengths as me why didn't you try and save yourself on this roof that day? Why did you think you were going to die?'

'Don't you realise it yet?' she shrieks in disbelief as if she still thinks of me as an ignorant child. 'If you aren't around I don't have the same abilities. I thought perhaps it was the guilt of what I had done, even though I didn't think I really felt any, but nothing ever came back. I was just a normal little girl again after you had gone, living out a normal boring existence. Been better if I hadn't let you drown that day, found some other way to get you out of my life. But die you did and you don't get to come back.'

'But I did come back,' I stare at her, challenging.

'Yes. Yes you did,' she nods and begins to pace around the roof, moving closer to me with each step. I want to move away from her but there is nowhere to go and the mists twist below me like the spectres of serpents waiting to swallow their next victim whole.

'I realised what you were trying to do the second time I woke up in that cottage by the way,' she continues, waving a finger at me like some TV detective explaining his deduction of who committed some crime. 'Do you know how frightening it was the first time? One minute I'm on this roof thinking I'm going to die. The next thing I know I am back in my childhood home and it is two months later. I didn't dare go outside. Didn't dare try to find out how I'd got there even. I think I must have just sat there for hours, rocking back and forth still convinced that Nathan had beaten me so hard I was in a coma somewhere and everything was an hallucination.'

And I can see what happened as she tells me; her waking up, staggering through the house, finding all her things, my things, her things, hanging in the wardrobe, lying on the dressing table, in the bathroom.

I see her look at her phone, turn on the TV. See the date. Try to remember how she got here but all the while the pain in her head is stopping her from thinking clearly at all. I see her then I am her. She snatches a piece of paper off the notebook by the phone, scribbles the note I found onto it, trying to make sense of what has happened to her, thinking if she writes it down it will become clear. That she can't forget again. I see her then I am her. And all the time the rain hammers against the windows just like the forecast said it would. And I feel her panic and confusion as she backs away from a world she doesn't understand until she is pressed up against the wall before sliding down it, her mouth open in a silent cry of despair, clutching at the packet of cigarettes but too weak to light one. And then it as if I am the one crouching on the floor and I can feel the hard wall against my back and it is my hand clasped around the small cardboard box and then I am just watching again. Like someone is switching between channels in my mind. I see her then I am her. I see her then I am her.

I see her then I am her.

'Are you listening to me Elena. Do you see what you did to me?

'Then the second time as crazy as it was I understood,' she says calmly, switching me back to the present, her complete control now jarring compared to the desperation I just witnessed, just felt.

'I somehow remembered what I had been doing when you'd forced me out of my own body. It was hazy like trying to remember a lucid dream or some weird ayahuasca trip which are so vivid at the time but then parts are so easily forgotten on waking. But this time I didn't forget, I remembered how busy I'd been trying to find ways to get back what was mine, how much I was capable of. But I was silly. I thought I'd won. I thought I was back for good and you were really gone this time, then once again I am watching you live my life. Watching you be happy. I had to do something about that.'

And I see her put the note about Will into the cigarette packet, knowing that I would find it, knowing that it would hurt me. Using him once again to get to me, just like she did all those years ago when it was him I thought I would find waiting at the lake for me.

She is right in front of me now. It is the strangest feeling, seeing her near to me. Looking at myself but not myself, at someone who is so different inside that the identical features seem to fade away, twisting out of recognition and leaving nothing but malice.

'So what now?' I ask

'Now?' she whispers, her face so close to mine that all I can focus on are her eyes, deep and hateful and burning revenge. She reaches up as if to cup my cheek and her expression falters for a moment as if she is truly pleased to see me again, her eyes filling with something reminiscent of kindness as they scan my face and she brushes back a lock of my hair as if it were an act of sibling tenderness but then they grow dark once more and the hate returns. 'Now you stay dead.'

And she grabs my shoulders, pushing me up against the rail of the roof. I reach back only just managing to keep my balance and not fall but she is clawing at my face now, at my eyes and hair and I know I have to get away from this ledge and away from her. And I should be feeling pain as I try and hold her back while she thrashes at me and then I realise I am feeling pain but not in the scratches she is making. It is deep within me as if she is clawing at my soul, ripping it apart, destroying all that I was, all that I am.

And then the guard rail is no longer behind me and I am falling but I manage to grab hold of the ledge.

Elsbeth smiles and crouches down in front of me.

'Time to give me back my life,' she whispers slowly digging her nails into each of my fingers as she peels them back, first the little finger, bending it impossibly far so that it is flat against the back of my hand then as I watch in horror she starts on the next one and again I don't feel the pain of the breaking bones and ripping tendons in my fingers but instead the agony is deep inside me and I cry out. The warmth around me that I know is Will clinging desperately on to my body, her body, in the real world is fading and I see her look around suddenly aware of his presence.

This is it. This is really my end. The agony inside me begins to subside, to become numb and as nothing as the void below me. Maybe this time it will be different and I shall truly cease to exist and I long for this for to watch her live now and know how much I have lost would be too painful. I would rather have oblivion.

And as I think this I lose my grip with one hand and nearly fall into the swirling fog below me.

Nearly.

But my other hand stays firm.

Because I want to live.

And I remember Will telling me what my aunt had believed.

That I am stronger than Elsbeth.

And I swing my free arm upwards, two of the fingers on my hand still hanging broken and useless but I manage to grab Elsbeth by the hair, pulling her forward.

And we both fall into the abyss.

Chapter 24

I hear Will's voice echo far away as if it is in a tunnel but I cannot reach it. I cannot reach him. I want to so much though, so much. I have to get back to him. I must. I promised myself I would spend the rest of my life with him and I meant it. I am not going to let him go now. I am not going to let him go ever again. But what if I have no choice? I try and focus on his words and I go to him but they are growing fainter. He is slipping away from me or am I slipping away from him? The words are just a whisper now but I hold onto them and all else drifts and melts into oblivion and then finally the words too fade and become just a memory.

And then all is gone.

Chapter 25

'Don't leave me Elena, please don't leave me. Not again. This isn't long enough. We haven't had long enough. I never told you I was sorry. I never let you know how much I love…'

The words choke in my throat as I cradle her in my arms. She is so frail and still, her head hangs back and her dark hair spills over my arms to the floor. I am too weak to help her. I was always too weak. I remember when I was ten how I had run to the lake after I heard what had happened, that one of the Reynolds girls had drowned, confirming what I already knew. I remember the mud coating my trainers and jeans as I fell to my knees on the bank and the cold and damp seeping through them. I remember trying to ignore the police tape fluttering around me, still attached to the twisted trunks. And I remember how I cried out to her, the birds taking flight from the overhanging branches as my scream echoed through them, ripping its way out of me and I don't know how long I stayed there, how long I whispered to her that I was sorry. Sorry for all the things that I had said, for all the things that I had done. I never meant them. I never meant a word of it and as I stared into the depths of the lake I wanted to let myself fall into it too, to follow her into the afterlife despite the memory of what it felt like to almost drown still fresh in my mind. It was not worse than this pain I was now feeling. Nothing could be. The wounds of my parent's dying were still open and sore but this new pain was something different. It was not just the loss but also the guilt. I could have stopped this. If I'd been with her she would never have been at the lake I knew she didn't like, or if she was I would have rescued her. At least I could have tried. I promised her I'd look after her. I promised I wouldn't let anything bad happen to her. I promised...

Instead I was on my own when she died, lying on the bed in my foster home, the curtains drawn and the room dark, staring at the ceiling, picking at a cut on my hand until fresh blood ran from it, only thinking about my own pain, my own suffering, never of hers. I still cared about her, however much I acted to the contrary. I couldn't stop caring about her. But she died believing that I did not. She died never knowing that I missed her smile, her laughter, the way she tucked her hair behind her ear. I missed the tiny wrinkle which would appear on her forehead if she was concentrating on something and the way she would push me and pretend to get cross if I teased her about it. Everything about her, I missed everything and I don't know why I couldn't have told her that. I don't even know why I acted like I did. I don't know why hurting her and pushing her away made me think things would get easier. Nothing got easier, nothing, and then I'd felt her go. I can't explain how but I felt it. A ripping inside me and a crushing in my chest like someone had placed a great stone there and was pushing down on it. And I struggled to breathe and I knew she was gone. But then I was told it was not Elena but Elsbeth who had died and I tried to believe it. I wanted to believe it. I even managed to fool myself for a while but I knew it was Elena who had been lost.

'I'm so sorry,' I whisper to her, the tears coming now as I search her face for a movement, a sign she can still hear me but there is nothing. Have I lost her again? Will she wake up as Elsbeth? Will she wake up at all? I shouldn't have lied to her or maybe I shouldn't have told her the truth. I don't know anymore. I don't know what is right and what is wrong. I don't even know what the truth really is. All I know is that the girl I spent the night with all those years ago was not Elena just as deep down I knew it wouldn't be. That was Elsbeth through and through. Selfish, hateful Elsbeth. But there was not a trace of Elsbeth in the girl who walked into that pub nearly two weeks ago, the girl dying in my arms right now. The girl I have fallen in love with all over again is Elena. I can't explain how I know I just do. Just like Carol knew I would. Elena who strange things happen around but I do not fear anymore. All I know is that I would give anything to have her back. I never dared to believe Carol. Never dared to believe I would get a second chance. I thought she was crazy and yet I always hoped that she wasn't. That what she said was true. That one day everything would be made right.

'Come back to me please! You have to wake up!' I shake her waiting for some response, some flicker that she is still there, that she is still my Elena, but there is nothing. Her skin is porcelain pale, fragile like one of the dolls in her old room upstairs and just like them I feel as if I let her go she will crack and break and never be the same again. And all the strength leaves me and I can't shout for her to hear me anymore and my voice becomes just a whimper and all I can do is beg. 'Please wake up. Please just come back to me.' I hug her to me and bury my face against her lifeless body. Her arms hang down limp and I can no longer feel her warm breath against me. The pain slices through me as I sob against her cold flesh. I have lost her again.

She is gone.

Chapter 26

Come back to me

The words float out of the darkness and I follow them to the light.

I feel the air rush into me, filling my lungs and my eyes fly open. I am on the floor of my aunt's cottage. How did I get down here? Will is holding me his face buried against my neck, crying. Why is he crying?

'Will?' I murmur and I feel him still, his sobs ceasing. He raises his head and looks down at me. 'I remember you.'

'Elena?' he gasps my name as if he dare not say it.

'She's gone.' The words come out without my bidding and I don't know who has gone or what I am talking about but before I can worry why I am so confused I see the pain in his face which is absolute. I feel his arms around me go weak as if I have just wounded him. 'Will?'

His expression becomes bitter, hateful.

'Elsbeth,' he spits, the tears falling unashamedly down his face.

'What? Will what happened? What about Elsbeth?' He studies my face now, his eyes questioning and then it is as if the sun has risen in them, chasing away the storm clouds which were there only moments before.

'Elena?' He swipes the tears from his eyes. 'It's really you?'

'Will, of course it is me, who else would it be? But what happened? Why am I down here? Did I fall?' I look around trying to recall what I was doing right before I found myself on the floor. The last thing I remember is that I was in the attic. I think I was looking in the old trunk up there but I can't remember what I found. Did I fall from the ladder? Down the stairs? Surely I would feel bruised if I had.

'No, no you didn't fall exactly,' he strokes my hair back, the tears still falling even though now he is smiling, laughing almost.

And his joy and tears are infectious because I start to cry and laugh too.

'Will what happened then? Why are you acting like this?'

He takes a minute to answer as if trying to process his thoughts.

'I thought I'd lost you again,' he tells me and the tears win against the laughter once more. Why would he think he had lost me? If I didn't fall did I have some kind of seizure? Did I pass out and stop breathing? I feel fine apart from I can't remember how I got down here and I try and sit up in his arms.

'Will I'm OK. You haven't lost me.' I don't know what is wrong with him or how to make him stop crying or what just happened exactly which got him so spooked so I reach up, cupping his face and kiss him to prove just how fine I feel. 'I'm OK,' I whisper.

And he presses his mouth to mine, desperate and hungry and relieved and although I know that I should be more worried about what just happened and what could have caused me to wake up on the floor with no recollection of how I got there, I am not. I know everything is going to be alright now and a peace settles over me which I haven't felt for years. He breaks away from my lips and his wide eyes stare into mine, shiny like blue sea glass as he searches my face as if seeing it for the first time.

'She's really gone,' he murmurs, his expression one of wonder and I don't know who he means and I don't know why I am on the floor but for some reason I say yes because I know that it is the right answer.

'Yes, she's gone.'

A beam spreads across his face and I don't know why I'm not more curious as to who has gone, or why I am answering questions I don't understand and then his next words make me forget to care about either.

'I love you Elena Reynolds. Did I ever tell you that?'

And I am six years old again and watching him spin in the falling blossom.

'No, but I've been waiting for you to say it for long enough.'

He grins, looking down shyly and I notice his cheeks colour before his eyes meet mine once more, this time his countenance serious. 'Don't leave me again OK. You promise me you're back for good, I don't mean in this area or county or whatever, I mean with me. Promise you're back with me for good.'

I reach up and stroke his cheek and he goes to kiss my palm as my hand sweeps up into his hair, swiping it out of his eyes as I've seen him do so many times.

'I promise,' I murmur and I mean it. I twist my fingers in his hair and pull him back to my lips because we have spent too many years apart and because today is the first day of the rest of my life and I am so happy to have found him again.

I am so happy just to be alive.

Chapter 27

My name is Elena Reynolds. I had a sister once, Elsbeth. She died. I tried to save her but I couldn't. Some people told me it was as if I'd died that day. That I became like her in some strange way to keep her alive in me. I don't know. I've always felt like just me. I still think of her sometimes and wonder if she's watching over me. I'd like to think so. I don't remember her that well now and we were never close but she was still my sister.

Epilogue

The little girl watched as the men in white plastic suits put up tents around the areas in the woods. She had already seen one body bag be taken away. A man had been found partially buried in the mud and debris about a mile into the woods though it did not look like he had been buried on purpose by any human but as if a wild animal had got at him and then discarded the remains. Several animals in actual fact for it was believed his eyes had been pecked out by birds and there were other lacerations on him as if foxes and badgers had also enjoyed their fill. A second man had been found caught in a trap which was even more of a concern as such things were banned. It seemed this must have been abandoned in the woods years ago, however, as roots had grown around it holding it fast to the ground, though how it had never been triggered before was a mystery. It looked like wild animals had got at him as well but it was unclear if it was only they who had tried to gnaw off his leg, for some of the bite marks looked alarmingly human and his own flesh was found in his mouth. The crime scene investigator conceded that the cold and being eaten alive could drive a person to extreme measures to try and get free. The third man was found drowned in the lake.

The girl was not particularly troubled by the scenes. She'd been in the woods over two weeks now and it was time to go home. She clutched the dirty grey rabbit closer to her as she stomped through the spring flowers, careful to stay off the paths, careful not to catch anyone's attention before getting onto the main road and then she hadn't far to go until she saw the house which was somewhat familiar to her.

It was the man who opened the door. He was tall, wearing a red jumper, his hair thinning with wisps of grey at the sides. At first he just stared at the girl before shouting to his wife.

'Susan! Susan, get here now.' The woman came to the door. Her eyes were red and her skin grey as if she had not slept for weeks for she had not.

'Grace?' she whimpered, pushing her still stunned husband out of the way. 'Grace?' And she hugged her daughter who had been missing for so long but she had never given up hoping even though with each passing day it seemed less and less likely she would be found alive. Finally the man came out of his stupor and also bent down to his daughter, holding her so tightly the little girl almost felt she couldn't breathe.

'Where have you been my baby? Where have you been?' the woman sobbed stroking the matted dirty hair from her daughter's face and then taking hold of her shoulders, waiting for an answer, waiting for her child to tell her she was not hurt, that no one had hurt her.

'I'm fine Mummy, a lady called Elsbeth was looking after me.'

'Elsbeth?' her mother frowned and then looked to her husband. 'John we need to call the police.' The man nodded and though reluctant to let go of his daughter went into the house to get his phone. The woman hugged the girl once more before taking her inside and going to her husband to see if he had got through to the police and what he was saying to them. The little girl stood still in the small hallway and looked around her new home. At the cream carpet on the stairs leading up to where she knew her bedroom was with all her toys, through the side door to the living room where a large TV stood, a stack of Disney DVDs beside it. At her loving parents crying down the phone to the police, telling them that she was finally found; that she was OK. And if anyone had passed by the open front door at that moment they would have seen her turn and smile before she closed it with just a glance.

Acknowledgements

Thanks go once again to Mike for his brilliant editing skills. Any general nonsense and mistakes are likely mine for continuing to tweak parts right up to publishing.

Thank you to Caz for all her enthusiasm; to Jo Old for several of the conversations with Sally which appear in this book and for all the Korev; to James 'The Library' Lorkin for his keen eye for great books and telling me he may take a chance on this one; to Lisa Gerrard for putting weird bells in her music and to Ryan Star for writing the song 'Losing Your Memory' which I just happened to be listening to when writing this.

And thank you to all the readers of my first book 'The Resonant' who encouraged me to write something else. Sorry this isn't the sequel asked for. That does exist but not ready for the world yet.

About the Author

Shauna Leone is an actress and writer living in North London with the diva dachshund, Summer Truffles. Her debut novel 'The Resonant' was inspired by her love of travel, pre-history and being very geeky about ancient sites while The New Home was written when living in Cornwall and spending a lot of time in the pub.

Printed in Great Britain
by Amazon